THE LOVE PROPOSAL

(A WEDDING DATE ROM-COM)

CAMILLA ISLEY

Boldwood

First published in 2020. This edition first publishing in Great Britain in 2023 by Boldwood Books Ltd.

Copyright © Camilla Isley, 2020

Cover Design by BNP Design Studio

The moral right of Camilla Isley to be identified as the author of this work has been asserted in accordance with the Copyright, Designs and Patents Act 1988.

Every effort has been made to obtain the necessary permissions with reference to copyright material, both illustrative and quoted. We apologise for any omissions in this respect and will be pleased to make the appropriate acknowledgements in any future edition.

A CIP catalogue record for this book is available from the British Library.

Paperback ISBN 978-1-83751-932-3

Large Print ISBN 978-1-83751-931-6

Hardback ISBN 978-1-83751-930-9

Ebook ISBN 978-1-83751-933-0

Kindle ISBN 978-1-83751-934-7

Audio CD ISBN 978-1-83751-925-5

MP3 CD ISBN 978-1-83751-926-2

Digital audio download ISBN 978-1-83751-927-9

Boldwood Books Ltd
23 Bowerdean Street
London SW6 3TN
www.boldwoodbooks.com

To all of us who've ever been tired of always being the bridesmaid...

1

SUMMER

Sterile and cold. The retrieval room is both. It's a compact space filled with medical equipment: a gynecological bed, an ultrasound machine, various monitors, and a metal IV stand.

As uninviting as the gyn bed looks, I fidget in my hospital gurney waiting for the nurse's permission to switch accommodations. I'm perfectly able to walk, but it's the clinic's policy to have me ferried between rooms this way.

Gosh, I hope this will be over soon. I've been second-guessing my decision to be here since the hormone shots began two weeks ago, and can't wait to be done. They said the procedure would take no more than twenty minutes, but I feel like I've been stuck in this room for hours, and we haven't even started yet.

The nurse must realize I'm fretting because she asks, "Are we waiting for someone to join you today?"

By *someone*, she means a partner. And the question is well-intentioned, I'm sure. Unfortunately, she's twisting the knife into the wound of my singlehood.

"No," I say. "I'm alone."

The automatic doors behind me swoosh open, sparing me the need to elaborate further on my lack of a love life, and two female doctors walk in. One is wearing white scrubs while the other is clad in salmon.

The salmon doctor speaks first. "Good morning. I'm Doctor Philips, and I'll be the one retrieving your eggs today. And this"—she points at her colleague—"is Doctor Mathison, your anesthesiologist."

The nurse hands the doctor my medical file.

Dr. Philips does a quick check of my record, and asks, "How are you, Miss Knowles?"

"A bit nervous," I say.

The doctor smiles. "No reason to be, Summer. Can I call you Summer?"

I nod.

"The procedure is quick, and you won't feel a thing." She gestures to the gyn bed. "Ready to jump?"

I nod again and, with the nurse's help, move onto the bed. The hospital gown I'm wearing flaps open as I stand up, but today's not the time for modesty. I lie in a half-reclining position with my back leaning at about forty-five degrees while Dr. Philips instructs me to please place my legs in the stirrups. And so here I am, half-naked, legs wide open, and completely exposed.

"Has the procedure already been explained to you?" Dr. Philips asks.

"Yes," I confirm. "But could we go over it another time, please?"

"Sure." The doctor smiles again. "First, I'll perform local anesthesia while Dr. Mathison will use an IV catheter to administer an intravenous sedative. Then, I'll use an ultrasound probe attached to a thin needle to make a tiny puncture through your vaginal wall and enter the ovary, where we'll suck out the fluid that encloses the eggs via the needle. And we'll be done in no time. Ready?"

For a needle to puncture my vagina? I'm as ready as I'll ever be.

I nod.

The doctor smiles once more and pulls on a surgical mask.

"Try to relax now," she says. "I'll start with the local anesthesia by administering four small injections. You'll feel four little pinches similar to what you'd experience at the dentist."

Ah, I disagree in my head, *but the dentist operates on my gums. You, doctor, are jostling around much more sensitive parts.*

The first pinch comes, and, okay, it's not bad. Honestly, the dentist analogy is strikingly correct. Anyway, I'm distracted from the second needle's prick by Dr. Mathison talking to my right.

She gently grabs the IV line, saying, "This is the pain medication. You might feel lightheaded, don't worry, it's normal."

I can only think, Hell yeah, please get me high before the big needle comes. Long live the drugs!

As promised, in a matter of seconds, my eyes cross and I feel insta-happy, not a worry to my name. I barely hear Dr. Philips say she's going in and, before I know it, I'm back on the gurney ready to be transported to my room.

Once there, the nurse helps me transfer to the hospital bed and instructs me to rest. She needn't have done so. With the sedative still running high in my bloodstream, the moment my head touches the pillow, I pass out.

* * *

Best. Nap. Ever.

I haven't slept so well in months and wake up only when the nurse comes back to check on me two hours later. She asks if I'm okay, and when I nod, she invites me to get dressed and wait for Dr. Philips, who will arrive shortly with my results.

I use the adjoining bathroom to get changed and, when I come out, Dr. Philips is already waiting for me, her usual friendly smile stamped on her lips.

"How are you feeling?" she asks.

"Good," I say, sitting on the bed—my legs are still a little like Jell-O. "The needle sounded scary at first, but I honestly didn't feel a thing."

"Happy to hear." The doctor nods, satisfied, and taps the medical folder in her hands. "I have your results here," she says. "The procedure was a success. We were able to retrieve seventeen eggs, of which fifteen were viable and have been frozen."

"Fifteen eggs? Is that good?"

"Fantastic. You're under thirty-five, and with this many eggs, you stand a 70 per cent chance of a live birth."

"Okay." I nod. Even if the pessimist in me can't help but concentrate on that 30 per cent chance I'll never have a baby.

The doctor must be used to her patients not being a cheery bunch because she doesn't comment on my scarce enthusiasm but continues to give me my prognosis. "Your body responded very well to the hormonal treatment, but one potential side effect of having produced this many eggs is that you're at risk of OHSS: Ovarian Hyperstimulation Syndrome."

That doesn't sound good.

"Luckily," the doctor continues, "the condition occurs only if you were to get pregnant, which"—she checks my file—"I see is not the case with you. We're not proceeding with fertilization, right?"

I know she's only doing her job, just like the nurse earlier, but, once more, it feels as if the doctor is purposely pointing out how single and desperate I am.

"No," I say. "No sperm donors on the horizon for now."

"That's fine. Frozen eggs, if properly conserved, remain viable indefinitely. And our facility is top-notch. We also offer a wide selection of donors in case you decided to proceed with fertilization later in time."

Again, she's just giving me my options. But I can't help feeling like a total failure, a woman whose sole chance of having a baby will be to pick a dad from a catalog because she couldn't find a man in real life.

The doctor finishes her report by giving me a list of medications I have to take for the next two weeks and mandating that I use protection were I to have sex.

Aha. Fat chance!

I've been in a dry spell for months and before that, the last man I had sex with ruined my life. Well, not just him; I played a big part in my own self-destruction. But still, I've sworn off men. Hence the need to freeze my eggs if I ever hope to have a family.

On that cheerful note, I thank the doctor one last time and leave the clinic. A few minutes later, on the street, I hail a cab to JFK.

*** * ***

At the airport, I clear the security checks super early. Unsure how long the procedure would take, I've kept a nice cushion and booked the red-eye flight back to LA.

With a couple of hours to kill, I could stroll the shops, but I'm not in the mood for shopping. Plus, with the anesthesia fresh in my system, I'm still a little groggy. I don't even have the energy to go look for a proper restaurant, so I settle for the first bar I find on my path.

I sit at one of the high stools at the deserted counter.

"Hey, you're back," the bartender—a friendly-looking guy with sandy hair and blue eyes—greets me as if we were old friends. He does a double-take and adds, "Not from the jungle this time, huh?"

What the hell is he talking about?

I stare, unsure how I should reply.

But the bartender just keeps going. "And how's the doctor?"

The doctor? How could he know I'm coming from the clinic? Do I have "sad lady who froze her eggs because she can't find a man" written all over my face?

"Did he find you?" the bartender asks.

He?

I blink, confused.

"Winter?" the guy asks, calling me by my sister's name. "Are you okay?"

And the mystery is solved: he thinks I'm my twin.

"Sorry," I say, smiling. "Wrong sister. I'm Summer. We haven't met."

The dude's eyes widen. "Oh my gosh, you look exactly the same."

"I know, identical twins and all... So, you've met Winter? When?"

"It must've been, what, almost a year ago now."

"Wow, you have a good memory."

He winks. "Part of the trade and your sister's story was too unique to forget. A treasure hunt, being abducted in the jungle by rogue militia."

"Yeah." I chuckle. "My sister never does things in half measures. Gave my parents a heart attack."

"Oh, well, she didn't seem too upset about the kidnapping. She was more concerned with the archeology professor leading the expedition not loving her. Winter told me her story when she grabbed some breakfast here before a flight, and after she left, what do you know, the dude in question showed up. He was brooding over a lost jungle love, and when I told him his lady had just left, he chased her halfway down the airport—guess he *was* in love. But I never heard how it ended."

"Well." I sigh, contrasting emotions swirling in my head—mushy joy, a bit of jealousy, and a boatload of terror. "He proposed two months later and they're getting married in three weeks..."

I hope I've kept the dread from my voice. I swear I couldn't be happier for my sister. But her wedding is going to span over a week to accommodate most of the groom's guests, who will fly in from all over the world. For Logan's friends, it wouldn't have made sense to travel to the States only for a weekend. And the bride and groom jumped at the opportunity to extend the celebrations to a full vacation.

And, normally, a week-long destination wedding in Napa would sound like a dream. I'd be looking forward to a break made of nothing but relaxation, wine tasting, and family time. While the celebration of love would be the cherry on top of my romance-loving cake.

But *this wedding*, I won't enjoy. All my ex-friends are invited. People who will stare, judge, and talk behind my back. The thought makes me want to crawl into a dark corner and never come out.

But I can't. For my sister, I'll put on a brave face, a fake smile, and trudge Monday through Sunday like a real soldier. Because Winter doesn't deserve to have my poor choices ruin the most important day of her life.

"Whoa." The bartender's smile is wide and genuine as he reacts to the wedding announcement; he hasn't picked up on my internal turmoil. Guess the past year has taught me how to pretend well. "Engaged and getting married in less than a year. That was quick," he says.

"Yeah, Logan is still working in Thailand most of the time, and a late-spring wedding was the only opening in both their schedules."

"I'm Mark, by the way." The bartender extends an arm forward. "Nice to meet you."

"Summer," I repeat, shaking his hand. "Nice to meet you, too."

"And sorry," Mark apologizes. "I've been monopolizing the conversation. What can I get you?"

I stare at the juicer machine behind him. "You make fresh orange juice?"

"Yes."

"An OJ, then, and a sandwich if you have any."

"We do," Mark says. "Is cheese and ham fine?"

I nod.

He prepares the food and puts the sandwich on the grill to heat. With the push of a few buttons, he sets the timer and moves on to the OJ, selecting two oranges from a metal basket above the machine and feeding them into the juicer.

Two minutes later, he puts a coaster on the counter and serves me my juice. "So," he says. "What brought you to The Big Apple? Business or pleasure?"

I wince involuntarily. "Neither."

Mark must notice my expression, because he says, "Sorry, I'm being nosy. It's a bad habit of mine. Guess it comes with the territory." He gestures at the bar surrounding us while he gets my sandwich out of the grill.

"No, don't worry." I take a sip of OJ. "It's just that I came to New York for a medical procedure. Something personal."

Mark frowns. "I'm so sorry, I didn't mean to intrude." The frown deepens. "Are you okay?"

Gosh, I'm such a moron. I mentally swat myself on the forehead. Now he's going to think I have cancer or something.

"Yes," I say, taking a bite out of the sandwich. "Totally okay." I swallow. "It was a *voluntary* procedure."

Mark studies my face, probably trying to decide if I had plastic surgery, but obviously bites his tongue and doesn't ask.

I blush and blurt out, "I had my eggs frozen, all right?"

Mark's eyes widen. "Oh, what clinic?"

Huh? Not the response I expected. "Why do you want to know? Are you an expert on fertility clinics?"

Mark smirks. "Sort of. My sister is a nurse at Clinlada."

"That's my clinic! I chose it because it was the most recommended on my insurance plan."

"And I can certify it's one of the best clinics in the country."

"What's your sister's name?"

"Gwen, Gwen Cooper. Did you meet her?"

The name doesn't ring a bell. "No, sorry, she wasn't my nurse." I twirl a lock of hair around my finger. "You think it's pathetic?" I ask. "Freezing my eggs?"

"No, it's smart. If you want a family but are..." He falters in his speech, most likely struggling to find a nicer way to say *a spinster*. "Not at a moment in your life when that's... err... possible. Cryopreservation is a wise move to protect your fertility and chances of having a baby when you're ready." He flashes me a goofy smile. "You can tell I'm a victim of my sister's propaganda, eh?"

Despite myself, I smile. I've told this guy, this total stranger, my innermost secret, and he's managed to put me at ease. Not just with him, but with my life's choices as well.

"You're right," I say. "And I'm not at a time in my life where a relationship is something I want to pursue."

"Busy with your career?"

"Yes, but it's not that." I chew off another bite before telling him the next part. "I've sort of sworn off men. I'm not ready to meet someone."

"Oh, honey, but that's the worst thing you can say if you don't want a man."

"Why?"

"Because the moment you stop looking, that's when Prince Charming will come knocking on your door."

2

ARCHIE

Three Weeks Later

Something is wrong.

Sunlight filters in through the blinds, piercing my closed lids. Plenty of light, more than there should be. But why is the excessive brightness an issue? I'm between jobs, which means I can sleep in even if it's Monday.

Still, I can't shake the feeling something is amiss.

I blink awake, already alert, taking in the entirety of my rented open-floor home in one eye-sweep. The house seems in order. No signs of a break-in, or a fire, or a gas leak. Nothing wrong there.

Next to me, a redhead stirs. Brittany, Tiffany, I can't remember her name from last night. We met in a bar as opponents in a game of beer pong. And I don't recall who won, only that we decided to move the celebrations to my place.

I peek under the sheets.

Yep! We're both naked.

Definitely nothing wrong with that!

Why hasn't the nagging stopped, then? The sensation I should be doing something else—*be* somewhere else—stays put.

I shake my head, dog-coming-out-of-water style, trying to clear my brain. I'm too old to play beer pong and still expect to wake up fresh as a rose the next morning.

Careful not to disturb Brittany/Tiffany, I slither out of bed and hop into the shower. No better way to regroup.

When I come out of the bathroom fifteen minutes later, wearing sweatpants and a clean T-shirt, the lady is still sleeping in the same position I left her in. She hasn't stirred.

Mmm. How to wake her without being unpleasant?

I settle on making coffee; the grinder is loud enough to raise an elephant. The beans' capsule is running low, so I open a new pack, top up the container, and switch my beauty on. Fancy coffee is a luxury I treat myself to, at least when I'm in a civilized place and note trudging around a jungle somewhere. The drip coffee maker with a built-in grinder was expensive, but worth its while. Nothing better than a pot of freshly ground java to start the day, whatever the hour. I make sure the water tank is full, turn the machine on, and wait for the magic to happen.

As predicted, the noise is enough for Brittany/Tiffany to stir awake. She rolls over in bed, blinking, and asks, "Is that coffee I smell?"

"Yep," I say. "It'll be ready in a minute."

She pulls herself up on her elbows, using the sheets to cover herself. "Mind if I use your bathroom in the meantime?"

"Absolutely," I say, and to give her some privacy, I turn my back to the bed, pretending I'm busy checking the machine.

I follow her movements around the apartment with my ears. The rustling of fabric, the padding of feet on the hardwood floor, and at last, the click of the bathroom door closing.

When Brittany/Tiffany comes back out—already dressed, I note with pleasure—I've just taken the first delicious sip of my superior Crema Arabica blend.

"Want a cup?" I ask.

"Sure," she says, sitting on a stool at the kitchen bar.

As I turn to grab her a clean mug, my eyes land on the couch and the half-packed bag lying open in its middle.

Shit!

I check the date on my watch, which confirms that, yeah, I'm screwed.

Logan's wedding is today. Well, not the actual ceremony, or I'd be a dead man. Thanks to my lucky star, the schedule only includes *one* meeting today. Starting tomorrow, the week will get busier and busier until the main event on Saturday. Guests will arrive between today and the next few days. But as best man, I'm supposed to get in the trenches with the first wave. And I have to report to the wedding planning marshal at four for a comprehensive debrief on all my best-man duties for the week. A destiny I share with the other wedding party recruits.

I stare at my watch again. Half past two.

Shit. Shit. Shit.

I make a quick mental calculation. From Berkeley to Napa, it'll take forty-five minutes on the bike. An hour tops if traffic is bad. If I hurry and skip breakfast or lunch—whatever my next meal would've been—I could still make it on time. But I have to finish packing and get rid of Brittany/Tiffany first.

"Hey," I say. "Actually, would you mind if I made that coffee to go? Sorry, but I just remembered I was supposed to be somewhere else like five minutes ago."

Brittany/Tiffany shrugs. "No problem."

"You need me to call you a cab or something?" I say, opening the cupboard above the sink to pick up a paper cup.

I fill the cup with steaming coffee from the pot, asking, "Sugar? Cream?"

"Black is fine," she says.

Great, she's making the goodbyes easy on me. I cover the cup with one of the plastic lids piled above the coffee machine and offer it to Brittany/Tiffany.

She takes it with a raised eyebrow, probably assessing the fact that I keep a stash of morning-after, to-go paper cups in my kitchen. Oh, crap. Is this going to turn into one of *those* mornings after? With shouting and accusations being thrown around?

But, stoic, Brittany/Tiffany raises her cup at me in a cheers gesture and takes a sip. Guess we were both clear last night wasn't about forever and ever.

"Sorry," I apologize again. "I really don't mean to rush you, but I'm running super late. Do you need me to call you a cab?" I repeat my offer.

She takes her phone out of her jeans pocket and unlocks it. "No need, I already called an Uber." She checks the screen. "It should get here any minute. I'll be out of your hair right away."

I round the kitchen bar and walk her to the door, where we both stop, undecided about how to say goodbye. Should we hug, kiss? We land on an awkward sideways hug, and Brittany/Tiffany is gone. Out of the house and out of my life.

I shut the door and rush back to the living room area, running around like a Tasmanian devil, mentally compiling a list of everything I have to bring with me:

Best man speech—hilarious, charming, and with a few tear-jerking passages for the ladies in the audience to swoon over—*check.*

Rented tux. Will pick it up at the location, will check off later.

Enough clothes for a week and a mix of casual and formal occasions? Nuh-uh.

Last night I only went as far as packing socks and underwear. A quick fix. I yank shirts at random from my closet, doing the best I can to fold them quickly but decently enough they won't get too wrinkled. I don't have time to make a conscious selection, so I overpack and have to struggle to pull up the zipper on my duffel bag.

But hey, packed bag—*check.*

I'm one step closer to making it to Napa in time.

I sling the bag over my shoulder, grab my bike keys from the nightstand, and stare at the apartment.

What else? What else? Am I forgetting something?

I don't think so.

That's when my gaze lands on the nightstand on the faraway side of the bed, and the red box lying on top of it half-open.

Condoms!

Damn, I can't believe I almost left without bringing a pack. I dash to the bedside table and grab the box, shaking it. Two measly plastic squares fall out. Not going to cut it for a week. Good thing this is only the first box out of the family pack I picked up last night. But where did I stash the rest? Let's see, I bought them at the CVS around the corner... I came home... dropped my keys in the hall...

I turn to check the small cabinet behind the door, and... *Bingo*.

Half a box went up in smoke last night, but I put all the remaining packs in my bag—one might say I'm being optimistic, but a good chunk of the guests will be single gals, so—and I'm ready to go. I do a last-minute check to make sure all electrical appliances are switched off, unhook my black leather jacket from the rack behind the door, and exit the house.

The bike is parked askew in front of the garage on my half of the driveway of the single-story duplex where I live. Guess last night I was in too much of a hurry to bother to park it inside, or straight. I don't own a car, so the garage is exclusive to the bike, whenever I take the trouble to store it indoors.

Which is almost never in the warmer months. My neighborhood is located near the University of California, Berkeley campus, in Berkley, and if the area isn't 100 per cent no-need-to-lock-your-doors safe, it gets pretty close.

I drop my leather duffel bag on the rear of the saddle and secure it in place with twin nylon straps. Then, I don my biker jacket and pick up my helmet, freeing it from where I've impaled it on one of the handles.

As I secure the clip beneath my chin, I can't help thinking I've forgotten something else. Something important. What is with me today? Are a few beers really enough to make me woolly-headed for half a day?

I rack my brain another time, but nothing comes up. And anyway, if I've really forgotten something, I can always buy a replacement. Napa is not the desert; the worst I risk is being ripped off by the local tourist pricing.

Half an hour later, I'm about to cross the bay over Alfred Zampa Memorial Bridge when a giant billboard catches my attention. In the ad, a beautiful blonde is flipping her bare ring finger with an annoyed expression while the caption reads: *She's tired of waiting*. In the lower right corner, a picture of a diamond engagement ring looms over the address and phone number of a local jewelry shop.

Something about the sign nags at me, but it's gone past in a heartbeat.

I'm already halfway over the bridge when it hits me: the rings!

In a panic, I let go of one of the bike handles to pat the inside pocket of my jacket. The box isn't there. Only one other place it could be: back at the house.

Shit!

Shit! Shit! Shit!

I'm going to be so late. Even if I use the bike to dribble through most of the traffic, the round trip will still take me at least another hour. No chances of making it in time now.

Logan will kill me, but not before Tucker—my other best friend and also the wedding planner—has emasculated me.

I open the gas and speed up as I finish crossing the bridge, then take the first available exit, turn my bike around, and merge again onto I-80 in the opposite direction.

When I finally ride up my driveway, I've barely killed the engine before I'm vaulting off the saddle, removing my helmet, and racing for the door.

Inside, the apartment is a mess, as per last night's activities and my hasty packing spree. Where the heck did I put the rings? I moved them around to be sure not to lose them, and now I can't remember where I decided they'd be safe.

Nightstands' drawers.

I open one, then the other.

Nothing.

I check my desk next. No red velvet boxes in sight on the desktop. And after a thorough search of all the drawers, I come up just as empty-handed.

A man on a mission, I proceed to systematically go through each drawer, cabinet, and container inside the apartment—bathroom and kitchen included—but I can't find the damned box anywhere.

I'm a dead man.

If they were regular wedding rings, I could just re-buy them. With a rush order, a week would be enough for them to arrive on time. But my best friend, being the sentimental archeologist asshole he is, chose a pair of antique, engraved gold bands that are impossible to replace. Just my luck.

At this point I'm sweating, half from the panic, half from the heat inside the house—I turned off the air conditioning before leaving. Also, a skipped lunch and almost sleepless night are catching up with me, and I still have another forty-minute to an hour drive north to make.

Sweat drips down my forehead and pools under my armpits; this leather jacket is suffocating. I tear it off and, on impulse, I open the fridge to stick my head inside. This feels amazing.

As I pull my head out, five long minutes later, something red catches my gaze. There, innocently lying on the middle shelf, is the ring box. How and why it ended up in the fridge, I'll never know, and I couldn't care less. I take it out, check that the rings are safe inside, and kiss it. I stash the jewelry in the leather jacket's inside pocket where it should've been from the start.

Domestic treasure hunt over, I check the time.

Ten to four.

So, I've found the rings, but I'm still neck-deep in trouble.

Even if I leave now, the meeting will be over by the time I arrive. No point in rushing. I might as well take another shower and eat before I go.

I fish my phone out of my pocket and compose a quick text to Tucker.

TO TUCKER

> Sorry, man. Something came up and I'm not gonna make it in time

> But I'll get there by tonight, I promise

Tucker's reply comes in the form of emojis. The first, a rolling-eyes yellow face, the second, a red pouting face with swearing symbols over the mouth. Guess I deserved that.

A second message chimes in.

FROM TUCKER

Drive slow on the freeway

And a third.

FROM TUCKER

And remember the rings

I type back.

TO TUCKER

Yes, Mom

My phone pings again.

FROM TUCKER

Anyway, if you get here at a decent hour, we'll be
in the Magnolia meeting room

I don't reply.

Did they book a meeting room to have an informal meet-up between the groomsmen and bridesmaids? Are they nuts?

And how long does Tucker plan to have the session last?

Thank goodness I accidentally got myself out of it.

This is going to be a long week.

3

ARCHIE

By the time I get to the hotel—more of a resort equipped with a pool, a spa and a vineyard in the backyard—in St. Helena, it's already a quarter to six. I ask the clerk at the front desk where to find the Magnolia meeting room, in case my friends really have gone insane and are still discussing dances, frills, and color schemes.

The man points me in the right direction and, after meandering along a few corridors, I find the designated room. A brass plaque outside the door identifies it as Magnolia.

I poke my head in and sigh in relief at finding the space empty. I'm about to leave to go check in when a phone starts ringing inside.

There's only one table in the room, and its polished wooden surface is clear of objects. Where's the ringing coming from? I follow the sound, kneeling down and crawling under the table where I find the device lodged between a chair and a table leg.

Without checking the caller ID, I pick up as I crawl out from under the table.

"Hello?"

"Oh, hello," comes a surprised man's voice from the other side. "Err, is Lana there?"

Lana, huh? She's Winter's best friend. Who, if I remember correctly, is dating Christian Slade, America's number one heartthrob and, until recently, Hollywood's most wanted bachelor. Could this be him on the phone?

And just because I'm an asshole, I say, "Sorry, who did you say it was?"

"Christian, her boyfriend." He confirms my deductions, sounding pissed enough.

An evil laugh plays in my head; it's not every day that one gets to mess with the so-called Sexiest Man Alive.

"Sorry, man," I say. "Lana left her phone."

"Where?" His tone has turned murderous.

And since I'm not a complete douche, I stop the teasing. "Meeting room. She must've dropped it while discussing flower arrangements or something. But mine is just an educated guess, unfortunately; I didn't get here in time for the wedding planning session."

"You sound devastated," Mr. Famous Actor says. I decide I like this dude. "And who are you?"

"Archibald Hill, the best man. Listen, man, I'll drop off your lady's phone at the concierge and leave a message to call you back, sound good?"

"Thanks, I guess."

We've barely hung up when a cute brunette pokes her head into the meeting room. Her long brown hair cascades past her shoulders in soft waves, and she's wearing one of those flowy maxi dresses in a pink flower print. She's missing a colorful band tied over the forehead, or she'd fit in perfectly with Berkeley's hippies of the seventies.

I dangle the phone in my hands. "Looking for this?"

Her deep blue eyes widen in surprise. "Oh, thank goodness it's here." Lana sighs in relief and closes the distance between us, taking the phone from me.

"Your boyfriend called," I inform her. "He wasn't too thrilled to speak with me. You should call him back."

Her eyebrows draw together in a curious frown as she studies me. "You must be the missing best man."

I grin. "How did you come to that conclusion?"

She smiles in return. "I've heard stories about you."

"Only good things, I hope?"

The smile turns coy. "Mostly about how my best friend had to save your ass, *literally*, and on multiple occasions..."

I chuckle at that. So, this sassy, no-bullshit attitude is to be expected not only from the bride-to-be but her friends as well?

"Touché," I concede. "What did I miss? Was the meeting really necessary?"

Lana gives me a long, glad-we-understand-each-other stare, and then smiles. "It was mostly a review of the schedule for the next few days and the mandatory events for the bridesmaids and groomsmen."

"Such as?" I ask, worried.

"Well, tomorrow we're going wine tasting, which is optional. Wednesday is dedicated to the bachelor and bachelorette parties, which you were supposed to organize for the bachelors" I snort. Tucker took care of that. "Planning the bachelorette party was one of my duties as maid of honor, too."

"Wait," I cut her off. "You're the maid of honor?"

She eyes me sideways. "Something wrong with that?"

"No, but... err... I assumed Winter's sister would be the maid of honor since she's family and all... Nothing personal."

Lana's face clouds. "Yeah, but we all had a fallout last year."

"I'm familiar with the backstory," I say, remembering Winter's ramblings in Thailand about how her twin sister had had an affair with their best friend's boyfriend. *This* woman's ex-boyfriend.

Lana seems taken aback, and blushes. "Winter told you?"

"The very first night we met." I chuckle. "Probably when she thought she'd never see any of us again once the expedition ended. And it's your fault Winter spilled the beans."

Lana scowls. "How is it *my* fault?"

"You made her promise to call her sister and indirectly stirred up all the feelings she ended up ranting about later. But I thought the Knowles sisters had patched things up."

Lana's frown relaxes. "They're in a good place now; we all are. But the role of maid of honor requires a lot of interaction with other people. All our friends..." She pauses as if searching for the right words. "...from before. And not everyone has forgiven Summer, so I guess Winter asked me to be the maid of honor to shelter her sister from blowbacks and unpleasantries."

"Makes sense." I nod. "Anything else important from the meeting?"

She checks a sheet of paper in her hands. "Not really. Thursday is a recovery spa day. Friday is free until the rehearsal dinner at eight. Saturday, the ceremony and reception. And on Sunday, it's over."

I low-whistle. "And you guys, what? Spent over an hour discussing this?"

Lana's lips part in a wide smile. "Well, Tucker got a little carried away with the minutiae." Then the maid of honor eyes me appraisingly once again. "If we could average out his fastidiousness and your devil-may-care attitude, we'd have two perfectly balanced groomsmen."

I link my arm with hers and steer Lana out of the meeting room. "I think we'll get along just fine. Any task regarding the best man and maid of honor specifically?"

She looks up at me. "Only walking down the aisle together, and joining the bride and groom on the dance floor for the first dance. Can you dance?"

I let go of her elbow, take her hand and guide Lana in a pirouette, saying, "I'm the master of the dance floor."

She chuckles. "Oh my gosh, Winter was right, you're such a flirt."

I wink. "Don't worry, I don't interfere with other people's relationships."

"Oh, I'm not worried."

I lead her down the hall. "So, when is the famous boyfriend going to join us?"

"Why? You want to ask for an autograph?"

"After the conversation we just had? He must be a fan already; he'll probably ask for mine."

"Why? What did you tell him?"

I grin from ear to ear. "Nothing at all."

We stop in the hotel lobby and Lana glowers at me. "I'd better call Christian back. See you later."

I give a mock military salute and watch her disappear down a corridor, her flowery dress billowing behind her in soft waves of fabric. Once Lana is gone, I turn to the concierge to check in.

Minutes later, I jingle the key to room 452, my lair for the next week, and turn toward the elevators the receptionist has directed me to. But before I can take a step forward, all the air gets sucked out of my lungs as I catch sight of Winter standing in the middle of the entrance hall, head bent as she checks her phone. Only, the bride-to-be is no longer the goofy, messy person I'm used to. She looks all put together in a skintight black dress with a low neckline. The hem of the dress reaches just above her knees, leaving the bottom half of her long, lean legs exposed. Even more outside her character, she's wearing a pair of black leather pumps with stiletto heels so high and thin... they're a kick right in my gut. But it's not just the shoes; her hair, usually a tangled mass of soft waves, is straightened to a silken golden-white curtain that hangs down to her waist.

Logan, my friend, you lucky bastard.

For the first time, the snake of jealousy coils in my chest and stands to attention for the woman before me. Yes, I made a pass at Winter when we first met, the same way I'd do with any attractive woman. But I never regretted our relationship turning into a solid friendship or her choosing Logan over me... at least until now. It's a primal, irrational instinct.

I shake my head.

Get a grip, pal.

How can I be jealous of my best friend for getting married when it's the last thing I ever want to do? Logan is about to give up his freedom; I sure as hell don't envy him that. He must be crazy to voluntarily put metaphorical shackles on his wrists. Because that's what the rings in my pocket are—handcuffs. But staring at the woman before me, I can't help but wonder... Is he really crazy?

Yeah-ha, dude. Come on.

No matter how formidable the bride, getting married in this day and age is folly. It has been since the certificate was no longer needed to have sex.

Conclusion made, I plaster a cocksure grin on my face and go greet the bride-to-be.

"Snowflake," I call.

She stares up at me, eyes widening, but before she can say anything, I'm crushing her into a bear hug. And I swear I didn't smell her hair, which might or might not have the most delicious coconut scent.

Instead of returning the hug, Winter tries to pull away. "Excuse me? What are you doing? I don't know you." Her hands land on my chest, pushing. "Let me go," she orders.

I obey, and take in her angry face, which is almost an exact replica of Winter's. *Almost* being the keyword here. This version has a slightly pointier chin and a narrower nose. Small, imperceptible distinctions, but that could make all the difference in the world and open an ocean of possibilities. And also explain my gut reaction to her.

"You're not Winter," I say. "You're her ev—er... twin."

Summer Knowles' eyes narrow. "Were you about to say *evil* twin?"

"No." I make big, innocent eyes.

"Yes, you were," she puffs, and then she starts hyperventilating while rambling to no one in particular. "This is perfect, absolutely freaking fantastic. As if having half of the people at this wedding hate me wasn't enough. Oh, no. My sister had to blab personal details of my life to the other half as well. So, *everyone* here can hate me."

I blink. "I don't hate you."

She refocuses on me and gives me a once-over. "But you judge. I know who you are. You're the missing best man."

I bend in a half bow, saying, "In the flesh; pleased to meet you."

"You can switch the charm off," Summer snaps. "My sister has warned me about you."

I straighten up and place a hand over my heart. "You wound me, and who's judging now?" Her mouth gapes open. *Ah-ha, gotcha.* I take advantage of her momentary lack of speech to continue. "May I still introduce myself?" And before she can say no, I extend the hand resting over my chest. "Archibald Hill."

She reluctantly takes it. "Summer Knowles."

A spark of electricity runs through me as our hands touch, and I know at that moment that I want her. It's a cliché, but true. I can feel it. The chemistry is there, inexplicable but real. Up close, she ignites in me the same gut attraction she sparked from across the lobby.

Our eyes lock, and I smirk. Summer lets go of my hand quickly, as if she's holding a hot potato, and returns my smirk with a subtle glare.

Beautiful *and* feisty. This is going to be fun.

"So, where is everyone?" I ask. "Do you guys have dinner plans?"

"You just missed them; Logan, Winter, and Tucker went into town to eat. But you might still be in time to catch up with them."

"And you're not going?"

"No," Summer replies, glacial, and before I can ask why, she adds, "Well, it was nice meeting you. See you around."

Without another word, Miss Uptight spins on her sinfully thin heels and stalks off in her tight skirt, hips swaying tantalizingly.

Oh, I will *see you around*, Summer Knowles. Nothing better to whet my appetite than a bit of a challenge.

* * *

Up on the fourth floor in my room, I drop off my bag, change into a clean T-shirt and sweatpants, and ten minutes later I'm already bored to death. I could call Logan and join the others in town as Summer suggested, but they must already be ordering dinner by now. Instead, I grab the remote and turn on the TV. I zap through the channels for something interesting to watch and land on ESPN. It's hockey night. The Stanley Cup final, game one, the Los Angeles Kings vs the Chicago Blackhawks.

This ought to be an exciting game. I might as well go downstairs and follow the match while enjoying a beer and a burger. I don't bother changing back into proper pants and am half-tempted to leave still wearing the hotel slippers, but that's where I draw the laziness line. I pull on a pair of white sneakers and head to the resort's sports bar.

As expected, the game is being shown on every TV screen around. What I don't expect, on the other hand, is the company. And what a wonderful surprise, I might add. The only other patron of the bar is seated on a high stool, impossibly thin stiletto heels wedged in the metal footrest, and a now-familiar curtain of white-blonde hair covering her entire back.

I grab the stool on her right, unleashing my most dashing smile. "Hello, again."

Summer turns to me and drops the burger she was eating onto the plate, licking barbecue sauce off her fingers. "Hi?" she says.

A question more than a greeting.

"Hockey fan?" I ask, sitting down and signaling to the bartender to come my way.

"Yes," Summer replies curtly.

We're interrupted by the guy behind the bar. "What can I get you?"

"A bacon cheeseburger with fries and a beer, please." I look at Summer's half-empty glass of red wine and ask, "You want another one?"

She studies me for a long moment and then nods almost imperceptibly.

I turn to the barman with a bright smile. "And another of the same for the lady."

"Will you be charging this to a room?" the barman asks.

"Yeah, room 452, please."

Summer is still studying me. "You know we're in the wine capital of the country, right? Shouldn't you try something local?"

"I'm sure the beer is going to be craft and from a fancy brewery nearby with a price tag to match."

Summer gives me a little smirk. "You're probably right." She raises her wine glass. "They're selling this for fifteen dollars a glass. Ridiculous."

"Is it good, at least?"

"No." She takes a sip, the hint of a smile curling her lips as she lowers the glass. "Good doesn't cut it. This is easily the best red I've ever had."

The bartender returns with her wine and my beer. The pint glass isn't branded, but the ale inside looks richer and denser than any run-of-the-mill commercial brew I've had. I take a sip to confirm my suspicions.

Yep!

Summer tilts her head toward me. "How about your fancy beer?"

I swirl the liquid in my mouth, pretending to be an expert taster. Mmm. If I had to describe it with one word, I'd say buttery.

Still, I wrinkle my nose, as any respectable beer snob would do, declaring, "Acceptable."

Summer gives me another playful smile. "Hard to please much?"

Four simple words that send another electric spark coursing through my body. All the hairs on my arms stand to attention.

I'm getting mixed signals here. Hot and cold. One moment she's the ice queen, and the next she's sort of talking dirty to me?

As if realizing she's been flirting, Summer lowers her gaze and takes another bite of her burger then studiously stares at the TV screen, avoiding eye contact. The move doesn't prevent me from me noticing the faint blush creeping up her cheeks.

Interesting.

This poses the question of which approach I should take. Should I be blunt, or subtle? Could I be both?

For now, I sense it'd be better to steer the conversation toward safer waters.

Something happens on screen and Summer groans. I stare at the TV; the camera is doing a close-up of a Kings player stuck in the penalty box.

"Did he deserve it?" I ask.

"Oh, yes, manual boarding." She pops the last bite of burger in her mouth and licks her finger. "But sucks anyway."

Finally, the bartender drops my food on the counter alongside a receipt. I sign the bill and take a bite out of a fry, asking, "Are you a fan of sports in general, or just hockey?" before digging into my burger.

"Only ice hockey. My ex-boyfriend got me into it and, well, he's long gone, but after following the Kings for over ten years the love for the game stuck. You?"

I chew down the first mouthful of my delicious burger, swallow, and say, "I'm out of the country too often with no reception to follow any sport. But I enjoy all the classics: hockey, football, basketball..."

"What about baseball? Isn't that *the* most classic sport?"

"Nah, baseball is only good for when I have jet lag."

Summer polishes off the last of her fries and cleans her fingers on a paper napkin. "How so?"

"Whenever I put on a game, I fall asleep within the first ten minutes. Pretty handy when you travel as much as I do."

She chuckles. "Guess you're right; baseball can be less than thrilling. Anyway, the only other game I watch is the Super Bowl, but I do it more for the fun commercials than the sport. I don't travel that much, so I don't need a jet lag fixer, but tell Winter, I bet she could use the tip."

"Hey, I never asked. What do you do for a living?"

"I work in a skincare company, in the lab. I'm a chemical engineer; I'm responsible for the formulation and development of the company's foundation line."

And just like that, an image of her in a scientist's white coat and nothing else but sky-high stiletto heels pops into my mind. I take a sip of beer and swallow. "A lab rat, huh? I wouldn't have imagined."

Pinning me with a stare, she asks, "And what would you have guessed?"

I can't voice any of the dirty, dirty thoughts swirling around in my head, but say, "I would've pinned you down as more of a front-end cat. Like PR or marketing. Event planning, maybe?"

"Heaven spares me, I'll leave that to Tucker." She smiles. "Poor bastard. How my sister and Logan roped him into organizing this wedding is still beyond me."

"Well, Tucker is our logistics man... so."

"Still, camping supplies and survival gear are a far cry from frills and flowers. He seemed so stressed at the meeting you skipped."

"Hey, I had an emergency."

Deep blue eyes pierce me. "What kind of emergency?"

I shuffle through the possible answers:

Option number one: A sleepover involving a redhead who made me work extra time last night and miss my wake-up call today?

Nah, buddy, the lady is already prejudiced enough thanks to whatever stories her sister has been feeding her, which I will have to investigate later.

Option number two: A slip-up with the wedding rings and their unexpected retrieval inside the fridge? Cute, self-deprecating enough. This is the way to go; I tell her the story.

Summer laughs. "The fridge, huh? How did the box end up in there?"

"I swear I still have no idea."

We chuckle again, and I'm happy to note she finally appears more relaxed. Nothing super obvious, but her mouth doesn't go taut the moment she stops speaking; her body language seems less rigid, and even her eyes have more of a spark. "But promise never to tell Tucker or Winter," I add.

"You bet," she says. "Anyway, you're lucky you missed that meeting. Tucker was super picky, and my sister... she's gone a little bridezilla."

"Has she?"

"Yeah, I know she's usually the laid-back queen, but getting married has made her obsessive."

"Is that why you didn't join them for dinner?"

Summer's easy-going expression darkens. "No," she says. "I just wasn't feeling that social." She stares at the counter for a long moment before adding, "To be honest, I can't wait for the week to be over. I'm dreading the next few days."

I don't know why she's opening up to me. It might be the wine, or that I already know about the skeletons in her closet. But I'll gladly use any breach into the mystery that is Summer Knowles.

"Because of what happened with Lana? I met her earlier, and she's cool."

"She's not the issue; everybody else is. My entire old circle of friends and my most judgmental relatives."

I wipe BBQ sauce from my mouth. "Are they being nasty?"

"That's what I'm expecting, but I haven't talked to any of them in months, so I don't really know..."

"Maybe they won't be as bad."

"Yeah, sure, and tomorrow the sky will part and unicorns will come galloping down the rainbows."

I swallow the last bite of my burger. "Sarcastic much?"

"Realistic. I foresee dark times ahead. I'm going to spend this week in isolation, and that's the optimistic outcome."

"Hey, we can be buddies if you ever feel lonely."

Summer picks up her glass, eyeing me with half a smile. "Are you propositioning me?"

"I'm single, you're single. I offer a week of great, no-strings-attached fun. But if you'd prefer to mope alone over spilled milk..."

She takes a sip of wine while studying my face, her eyes lowering to my mouth.

I'm already thinking I have this in the bag when she says, "Thanks, but no thanks."

My expression must crumble, because Summer adds, "Oh, please, don't sad-dog me; I'm sure you'll find another hookup by tomorrow night."

"May I ask why the hard pass?" I make a half-cute, half-dismayed pout. "Am I not handsome enough?"

"Oh, you're very handsome." She finishes the wine and places the glass on the counter. "But I don't have to tell you that, right?" Her eyes return to my mouth. "Even if I've never much cared for"—her hands waver in the general direction of my chin—"facial hair."

"You mean my beard?" I exclaim, pulling at it. "Ladies all over the world have loved it."

"And that's the other thing. Lately, I'm trying to make smart decisions—"

"And smart and fun are mutually exclusive in your vocabulary?"

"I've slept with a total of three men in my life—"

"I'm sorry, how old are you?"

"Twenty-nine going on spinster, why?"

"How did you manage to sleep with only three dudes?"

"Easy, I was with the same guy high school through grad school—"

"The hockey fan?"

"Him, Robert. Then I had a bad rebound, followed by an even worse one that ruined my life and after that, I swore off men and am enjoying a protracted celibacy." She raises her glass in a mock toast and tilts her head appraisingly. "While you, you've probably slept with as many women in the past month, if not more. This arrangement you propose wouldn't carry the same weight for both of us." She extends a hand toward me. "Friends?"

I groan. "What is it with the Knowles sisters and just wanting to be my friends?"

Summer smiles. "Genes?"

I take her hand, not yet ready to accept defeat. As I get up, I pull in close to her, bending down to whisper in her ear, "I'm in room 452 if you change your mind. I can make you forget your name if that's what you need to get through the week."

4

SUMMER

Archie's breath is a warm caress down my neck. I swallow, trying to keep it together. No man has touched me in months, and my skin is singing at the unexpected attention. Tingles shoot up my arm from where our hands are joined, and having his mouth so close to my ear is making my entire body heat up.

With such proximity, I can smell Archie's scent. A mix of clean soap, an expensive citrusy perfume, and bare masculinity.

I swallow and meet his stare made of icy blue eyes now crinkled with mischief.

Another whispered word, another touch, and I'll beg him to bring me to his room and make me forget my name. But thank goodness, he doesn't add anything. The best man nods in farewell as he lets go of my hand and walks away toward the elevators, looking unfairly hot for someone wearing sweatpants.

Yeah, staring at his round behind bobbing down the hall won't help me stick to smart choices, so I look away.

My gaze lands on the entrance's revolving doors where, to my horror, two of my ex-friends, Susan and Daria, are walking into the hotel, carry-on luggage in tow behind them.

The first ghosts from my past have arrived.

I turn my face away, wishing I had an invisibility cloak under which to disappear. Or, to be more pragmatic, that I had a beanie to conceal my hair at least. I love my long, white-blonde locks, but the mane is hard to miss. In a panic, I pick up my bag from the counter and ask the bartender where the restrooms are. The man points me to a hall to the right with a toilet sign above it. I hop off the stool and follow his directions. I've already signed the receipt and won't need to come back to the bar. And to go back to my room, I can find another set of elevators or take the stairs, steering clear of the lobby.

Down the hall, I push the bathroom door open and hide in a stall for good measure. Ugh, this is the worst. Despite my best efforts to come prepared—meditation, yoga, even therapy, I can't ignore the icy dread that creeps up my spine as I realize what I'm about to face. A week trapped in a hotel with all these people I never wanted to see again and would rather forget. How am I going to survive this?

Avoiding two of them for an evening won't solve the problem, especially since I can't ditch any of the events or I'd be spoiling the celebrations for Winter. Before coming, I was aware I'd have to deal with my past, but the real-life experience is worse than I expected. I'm not ready for the panic and shame assailing me even without a face to face. What about when I'll be forced to really confront them? I'm going to die of mortification.

I close my hands into tight fists, digging my fingernails into my palms, and sag against the metal door to stare at the ceiling. Two glasses of wine should've helped me relax, but no, I'm still a bundle of nerves. And if a little liquid courage can't even help me chill out, this week is going to be truly horrible.

The bathroom door swings open, and Susan's voice drifts in. "Couldn't you wait until we got up to our room?"

"Sorry," Daria's voice replies, getting closer. A door bangs next to me. "It was a long drive, and you've seen the line at the check-in."

On alert, I push away from the stall's door and backtrack to the rear of the tiny space, hoping my feet won't show underneath. Could they recognize me from my shoes? I doubt it.

"Whatever," Susan says, her voice closer now. I can picture her staring in the mirror while bouncing up the edges of her short bob of brown hair. "Are we going out tonight, or are you tired?"

"I don't know," Daria says. "You?"

"I texted Winter; they're downtown at a French brasserie."

"Who's 'they'? Is the scarlet woman going to be there?"

Blood turns to ice in my veins; she's talking about me.

"Probably."

"Yuck." After the longest time, Daria flushes and comes out of the stall. "Then it's a pass for me."

"You're still that mad at Summer?" Susan asks. "If Lana could move past—"

"Lana is an angel fallen from heaven," Daria interrupts, turning on the water to presumably wash her hands. "I'm not."

Susan must make a face, because Daria says, "Susy, drop it."

"Okay, I will, if..." A pregnant pause follows. "If you explain why, just once."

The sound of paper towels being yanked from their container on the wall is the only noise that fills the room for a few unbearably long seconds. In the ringing silence, I'm scared they'll hear the pounding of my heart against my rib cage.

"What difference does it make?" Daria asks.

"I hate that our group fell apart and disintegrated. We were so close, the seven of us, and now it's just you, me and Martha most of the time. And I'm not saying I don't love hanging out with you both, but it isn't like before."

When Susan says the seven of us, she's talking about them, plus me, my sister, Lana, Martha, another regular in our group, and Ingrid, who's the wife of Johnathan's best friend, Mike. The moment the affair became public, Johnathan and I were sort of cast out, and Mike stuck with his buddy, leaving the group and pulling Ingrid along. But I had no idea that even Winter and Lana didn't hang out as much with Susan, Daria and Martha anymore. I'd just assumed I'd dropped off the invite list to their nights out.

"Sorry, sweetheart, but the group will never be the same," Daria says. "That ship sank when little Miss I'll Go and Screw My Best Friend's

Boyfriend torpedoed it by having an affair with Johnathan. I still don't understand how Lana found the strength to forgive her, but I never will."

Daria's last words cut through my heart like a blade.

"But why? Summer didn't steal *your* boyfriend."

"Susy, she was my best friend. Summer supported me when Tom had the affair, and then Gabriel. She witnessed firsthand what being cheated on did to me, how destroyed I was. Now, tell me, what kind of cold-hearted bitch would consciously unleash all that pain on another woman, let alone her supposed best friend?"

The blade continues to slice through my already-injured heart, filleting it to shreds. What I did to Lana was wrong, inexcusable. And Daria's right: I didn't deserve Lana's forgiveness, or hers, or anyone else's.

"No, no, you're right," Susan says. "She's a total bitch."

I cringe in my corner, flushing in shame.

"Lana got lucky she fell into a new relationship straight away, but she could've been broken to the point of no return," Daria continues. "I've learned my lesson, and Summer Knowles is the kind of toxic person I don't need in my life, thank you very much. And besides, she hasn't had the guts to send me a single text since she was outed."

"Yeah, me neither," Susan says. "Honestly, I don't know how she's going to show her face around this week. I mean, *everyone* knows."

Thank you, Susan, for pointing that out. As if I wasn't worrying enough already. Susy is one of the most good-hearted people in our group, and if this is what she thinks of me... Anxiety twists in my stomach, and I fight hard to choke down a sob in my throat. They can't find out I'm in here, hiding and eavesdropping on everything they say.

"Serves her right," Daria snaps. "Let's go."

Wheels roll on the floor, and the washroom door is pulled open.

"Speaking of Lana's new relationship," Susan says, her voice moving away. "I have it on good authority Christian Slade will come to the ceremony. He should arrive by Thursday or Fri—"

The door slams shut, and Susan's voice gets cut off.

After they've left, I wait another ten minutes before coming out of the stall, in case they forgot something and bounced back in. When I exit, I'm half-stumbling and need to steady myself by bracing my arms on the marble sink. Their words hit me worse than if they'd taken turns punching me. They despise me. And I deserve every ounce of their hatred. Everything they said is true. I did wrong by Lana, and no apology can make up for it. No matter what I do or don't do, I can't change the past. I can only try to be a better person in the future.

I take a hard, long stare at myself in the mirror. My eyes are bloodshot, but I managed to keep the tears in. Still, my skin looks pasty, except for the bluish bags under my eyes. Taking a deep breath, I run my fingers through my hair and let the silence wash over me like a bath of healing water.

It doesn't work though; the pain lingers like an open wound that will never heal, reminding me of what a terrible person I am. In the back of my mind, I know that, despite everything that happened with Lana, despite her forgiving me, forgiving myself will be the hardest thing yet to do.

But for now, all I can do is try to keep my head up and face what lies ahead—the upcoming ceremony and the brave face I must put on for my sister's sake. If only people knew how much courage it took to just get out of this restroom...

But fear is useless. Fear of being alone is what landed me in this situation in the first place. How ironic that because of that fear, I ended up being lonelier than I've ever been in my life. Because for the first time, I messed up so badly that even my twin sister—who's always been like an extension of me—couldn't bear to look at me for months and took forever to forgive me.

I know I should be brave and just ignore the snark, but at this moment, I'd give anything to be anyone but myself, to not feel trapped in my own skin, in my past mistakes. Heck, to be honest, I'd settle just for a good night of sleep without being tormented by my own guilty conscience. By the friendships I ruined. By the trust I broke. By the lies I told.

I splash some water on my face and take a deep breath. I just need a way to forget and move on. To ignore the dirty looks and harsh critics. Believe me, people, no one judges my past actions harder than I do.

I look into my red-rimmed eyes again. One week. Six nights. All I need is to find a way to pull through. Then I can go back to my lonely life in LA, bury myself in work, and forget I used to be a happy person once.

That's when Archie's words echo in my head.

"I can make you forget your name if that's what you need to get through the week."

I shake my head and splash more water on my face, trying to clear my mind.

Sleeping with the best man would be another bad decision with *huge mistake* written all over his sexy, crinkly eyes.

Still, part of me is tempted to take him up on his offer. To forget everything and just be in the moment with him. But another part of me knows that a fling with Archibald Hill would just be a temporary fix. I can't keep running from my problems forever.

Well, not forever, I reason.

I only need to make it through the week, I remind myself. Yes, he'd be only a Band-Aid on a deep wound that needs stitches, but he'd get me through the week at least.

"I don't know how she's going to show her face around this week. I mean, everyone knows."

Yeah, no. I can't make it through the week alone. Am I being self-destructive again? Maybe, but I need the distraction.

Steeling my nerves, I take one final deep breath and then make up my mind. *Alright, Archie, let's see what you got.*

I grab my bag and storm out of the bathroom, heading straight for the bar.

Archie is no longer at the counter, of course, but I need a little extra liquid courage before taking him up on his offer.

Not bothering to sit again, I wave at the bartender to attract his attention.

He comes my way at once. "You wanted something else?"

"A shot, please."

The bartender eyes me slightly too long before asking, "Any preferences?"

"Whatever," I say. "Make it strong."

He nods and gets pouring.

When he puts a tiny glass in front of me a minute later, I don't even ask what's in it. I raise the glass to my lips and tip my head backward, downing the liquid in one swallow. *Vodka.* The alcohol burns my throat and makes my eyes water. I do my best not to let it show, and drop the empty shot glass back on the counter.

With an annoying smirk stamped on his lips, the bartender asks, "Another one?"

"No, thanks," I say. "One is fine. Put it on room 452."

I don't wait for the bartender's response, but head straight for the elevators. The best man is about to get lucky; the least he can do is buy me a drink first.

"Don't worry," the bartender calls after me. "This one's on the house."

I ignore him and step into the elevator.

The ride up to the fourth floor is short enough to prevent any second-guessing, and in no time, I'm standing in front of room 452 knocking on the door.

5

SUMMER

Archie opens the door a few heartbeats later without even asking who it is. His face barely registers surprise at finding me standing on his doorstep.

Bastard.

He hasn't changed clothes, except that he is now wearing hotel slippers instead of sneakers. The new ensemble should be ridiculous, but the prick looks even more handsome.

Arms crossed over his chest, he leans against the doorframe with a smug smile curling his lips. "What can I do for you?"

I don't have the will to play cat and mouse, so I cut to the chase. "I'm ready to forget my name."

Ice-blue eyes study me, X-raying me through to my core. Until, finally, Archie steps aside. "Come on in, then."

I walk into the room, the door closing behind me with a loud click. This is it, I'm in. No turning back.

Archie is still studying me, and I can't withstand the scrutiny. So, for lack of better alternatives, I throw my arms around his neck and kiss him.

This is the first time I've kissed someone with a beard, and it's not what I expected. The hairs are soft and a bit ticklish, but leave the full lips underneath 100 per cent enjoyable.

At first, he doesn't respond, probably taken aback by the suddenness of it all. But then he commits and kisses me back, already making me forget my name a little.

His hands brush past my waist, settling on the small of my back as his lips move slowly against mine, deepening the kiss only for a tortuously short moment before he pulls back.

"Whoa, whoa, whoa." Archie holds me at arm's length. "Are you drunk?" he asks, probably tasting the vodka on my lips.

"Don't worry, I had one shot." I raise a single finger. "You're not taking advantage."

I try to kiss him again, but he tilts his head backward and upward, away from me. Then he gently removes my arms from around his neck, and, still holding my wrists, places our joined limbs between us like a barrier.

"Sorry," he says. "Not how this is going to work."

I frown, confused. "What? You have a no-kissing policy?"

If that's the case, I'm leaving faster than the Road Runner from Wile E. Coyote.

Beep Beep!

"Oh, no. We're going to kiss," Archie says, and I relax and tense at the same time. "Just not yet."

"Why?"

"Something happened downstairs that made you so worked up you downed a shot and came up to my room half an hour after swearing you wouldn't touch me with a ten-foot pole."

I hate that he can read me so well when he doesn't even know me. "I'm entitled to change my mind."

"So am I."

"If you don't want to do this anymore, I can just go."

He shrugs. "I'm just not up for angry sex. Not that it doesn't have its merits, but not tonight."

My jaw drops. This guy is so arrogant, so full of himself, so—

"I want you to have a clear head before anything happens," he adds, smoothing the tension. "That okay?"

I was about ready to get the hell outta here, but he's pulled me back in.

"What do you propose?" I ask.

"How about a foot massage, to start?" he asks, and, eyeing my shoes, adds, "Those stilettos must be killing you."

The heels are uncomfortable, but... "A foot massage?" I ask. "I thought we were going to do something a little more *daring* than that."

Archie's thumbs circle over my wrists, which he's still holding, letting me know everything this man does with his hands is *dicey*. "I promise," he says, his grin growing more wicked, "it will be the dirtiest foot massage you've ever had."

That, I can believe.

With my mouth already a little dry, I nod.

"Let's go outside. The night is warm, and I won't even need to put on ambient sounds."

He guides me across the room, then lets go of my hands to open the French doors on the other side. The balcony is a photocopy of mine: fifteen feet by ten, furnished with a table, two chairs, and two chaise lounges, all in brown plastic wicker.

Archie gestures to one of the recliners and I lie down on it, kicking my shoes off as soon as my feet lift off the floor—gosh, these pumps are real killers. As I ease back on the cushions, my black dress rides up my legs, showing a quantity of skin I'm not usually comfortable with. The fact doesn't escape my host's eyes, and he throws my exposed thighs a hungry look. Well, pal, you're the one who wanted to waste time with stupid foot rubs. He turns the other chaise lounge so it's perpendicular to mine and sits on the edge, patting his thighs expectantly.

I give him my right foot.

Warm, dry hands swallow my foot in their grip. Either my feet have shrunk, or his hands are really big. The moment his fingers start to move in slow, soothing circles, I relax against the back of the recliner. Despite my initial reservations, I close my eyes and let out a moan of appreciation. Maybe a foot massage wasn't such a terrible idea.

Until the masseur disrupts my quiet enjoyment by starting to talk.

"So, are you going to tell me what sent you bolting for my room?"

I lift a single eyelid. "Actually, I was planning on enjoying my massage without having upsetting conversations."

"Sorry, I play by different rules."

"Really?" I turn my full attention to him. "When you promised me a week of fun, I thought the purpose was for me to forget about my problems, not to get the third degree about them. Isn't the whole point of a no-strings deal to keep everything on a surface level? Why do you want to know?"

Archie rubs my heel, and it feels so good I might accept playing by his rules. "You're a riddle, and I'm curious."

"A riddle, how?"

"I know your sister pretty well, and you're nothing like her."

"Just because we look the same doesn't mean we *have to be* the same."

"No, okay. But you don't seem like someone who would—"

"Stab her best friend in the back? Have an affair?" I offer, a bitter smile parting my lips. "Admittedly, those weren't in my thirty before thirty list of things to do."

"So, what happened?"

"Would you believe me if I told you I'm not sure?"

"What do you mean?"

"I dated the same guy throughout high school, college, and grad school. He asked me out junior year when dating was all about meet-cutes, school dances, big feelings, and forever. No online dating. No apps for hookups. Fast forward to over a decade later and the romance world had gone to Tinder, Bumble, Hinge, Asparagus, or whatever dating app is the flavor of the month. I went from talking about marriage and kids to trying to avoid receiving unsolicited pictures of strangers' genitalia."

Archie chuckles. "I'm pretty sure there's no dating app called *Asparagus.*"

"This isn't funny. I spent months running into guys that... Well, guys like you."

"You mean handsome and dashing?"

"In part," I admit. "It's not that hard to find a pretty face. But they were all interested in a hookup and nothing else. Like two weeks was the standard max expiration date for a relationship. I woke up in a world where talking about commitment before forty was sacrilege." I stare at the dark sky and twinkling stars, listening to the crickets in the grass. The warmth of Archie's hands on my feet keeps me from shivering as the night turns chillier. "I made a point not to be swallowed up into that high-churn madness."

"How?"

I smile bitterly. "Easy, I didn't put out on the first night, or the second, or the third. But then of course, none of the guys stuck around long enough. And the only one who did..." I shake my head at the memory that still stings. "Never bothered to call me back after he got what he wanted. It was enough to convince me I'd never meet anyone, that I'd die alone with the proverbial ten cats."

"And how did that translate into sleeping with your best friend's boyfriend?" Archie asks, with no judgment in his blue eyes, just genuine interest.

"We ran into each other, had lunch, and it was... unexpected, easy, fun, safe. New but familiar at the same time. Like what I'd imagine it'd feel to discover you suddenly have feelings for an old friend. And I mistook being comfortable for being in love. That's when the envy started and when a darkness I didn't know I had in me bubbled to the surface. Why couldn't Robert have loved me the way Johnathan loved Lana? Why did my ex have to break my heart? Why couldn't I be more like my sister, happy on my own without the need to be with a man to function?"

Archie doesn't talk; he lets me get the things I haven't told anyone, even my therapist, off my chest.

"I was spiraling down that vortex when Johnathan started texting me in private, outside of our group chat. That's when the real ugliness started, and I came up with a million excuses to justify replying to him. We weren't doing anything wrong. It was just texting. Perfectly innocent, right? But then he started telling me how he and Lana hadn't been in a good place for a long time, that he wasn't sure he loved her anymore. Selfishly, I told him that if that was how he felt, he should break up with her. But he had a million reasons not to. It's complicated; we've been together a long time... One afternoon we were meeting up for coffee, and he tried to kiss me. I shoved him back, telling him I could never do that to Lana, that he should stop texting me, that I never wanted to see him again."

"Guess that didn't stick?" Archie asks, still no judgment in his voice.

"He was at my door two nights later, swearing he was in love with me.

That's what did it. My need to feel loved by someone, anyone, to know that I was desirable and wanted. And in that moment, nothing else mattered. After, I felt like shit, but ironically, that was also what made me continue the affair."

"Why?"

"Because if I could do something so horrible to my best friend it had to have meant something. It must've been true love. And so I started giving myself new justifications. Johnathan and Lana were wrong for each other, nothing should get in the way of true love, she'd be better off with someone else..."

"Which she ended up being."

"Yes, but I wasn't doing Lana any favors. I may have been caught up in the idea of love, but I was still aware that my actions were wrong. I was being selfish, full stop. I was doing whatever I wanted to do at that moment, so desperate I was to feel a connection, and damn the consequences."

"Doesn't sound like the worst way to live."

"Ah, but then you really have to not care about the consequences, 'cause karma is a pesky bitch and it catches up."

"Has it?"

The same pain and shame that wrecked me when Johnathan called to announce Lana had found out about us hit me in the gut as if it happened only yesterday. Winter disowning me as a sister. The fallout with all my friends.

In the end, Johnathan didn't even choose me. We were found out, and he came to me because it was the easier road. The only road he had left at that point probably. And then he further belittled whatever shameful ugliness we shared by selling our story to the press to make a few quick bucks and to get back at Lana for moving on so quickly. Oh gosh, the moment I realized he never even loved me, that I'd thrown my life to hell for nothing comes crashing back down on me now. The memories all swirl in my head, making me dizzy. Anxiety builds up in my chest and my hands go clammy.

"You're depressing me," I say, trying to claim my foot back. "I should go."

I try to pull my leg, but Archie keeps my ankle hostage in his hands. "Nuh-uh, sorry, my bad. No more sad topics." He circles his thumbs under the sole of my foot in a motion so sublime it threatens to make my eyes roll into the back of my head. I can't help but sink back into the chaise lounge and relax.

"What did you think of the beard?" Archie asks casually as if we hadn't spent the last half an hour discussing the darkest stains on my past. "Was it that horrible to kiss?"

I can't help it; my lips curl up in a smile. This guy is something else. "I thought it'd be worse, but I'm not convinced I like it yet."

He grabs my other foot and starts to give it the same delicious treatment as its predecessor. "By the end of the week you'll be a fan, I promise."

He winks, and my stomach responds with a little flick because those eyes... they're just so captivating.

I chuckle. "Oh, so only hipster boyfriends in my future?"

"I'm not a hipster," he retorts.

"And I'm not posh," I say with self-irony.

Archie smiles. "Fair enough."

I stare into his ice-blue eyes, which are filled with mischief. "So, Mr. Hill, your turn to share. What's the worst thing you ever did?"

His smile turns wicked. "Oh, baby, the night isn't long enough for that list."

"Don't call me baby."

"Okay, *Summer* Knowles, I won't."

"You haven't answered my question... the worst thing you ever did?"

"Never said I'd answer questions."

"So you take but you don't give."

"I give plenty, don't worry."

I feel the words like warm honey flowing low in my belly. Still, I ignore the innuendo and prod him further. "Give me one thing and make it serious, no jokes, no deflecting."

His eyes smolder. "I've never been in love."

With what my sister told me about his licentious habits I don't find it hard to believe. "Have you ever given yourself enough time to fall in love?"

"Maybe not."

"Do you regret it?"

"The way I see it, I've had it easy. No heartbreak, no unnecessary complications."

"And don't you ever long for a deeper connection, for something that doesn't flare up and burn in a night?"

He shrugs. "I have my friends for that."

I look away. "Maybe you're right and it's just a dog-eat-dog world out there; better not to get attached."

"That doesn't mean you can't enjoy the fire while it lasts," he says, his voice dropping an octave.

I turn to face him again. Our eyes lock. Hold. Then his movements on my foot shift, oh so slightly. I wouldn't be able to explain how, but they become more suggestive, more sensual. As if every touch has a sexual double entendre. Electricity tingles up my leg—and it's just as well I'm lying down because my knees turn to Jell-O. This is officially the dirtiest foot massage I've ever gotten. Makes me wonder if the man can deliver on *all* his promises.

As if reading my mind, Archie lets go of my ankle and stands up, offering me a hand. "You're ready to forget that name of yours."

I swing my legs off the recliner, sitting with my back straight, and look up at him. I take his hand and let him pull me up and into the room... ready to make my next mistake.

6

ARCHIE

As I pull Summer into the room, I can't help but notice how her eyes dart across the space as if looking for an escape route.

I trail a finger down her upper arm. "We don't have to do anything you're not comfortable with."

She looks at me, eyes blazing. "Aren't you supposed to be a bad boy? Are you always this gentle?"

To be honest, I'm not. But the Tiffanies and Brittanies I sleep with usually are more blasé about casual sex and aren't the vulnerable sister of a close friend. Summer is an adult and can make her own choices, but I want to make sure the choice is hers and hers alone, and that I'm not pushing for something she doesn't want or will come to regret.

I smirk at her, letting my hand trail down to the curve of her waist. My hands settle on her hip bones and I begin drawing lazy circles with my thumbs. "You don't want gentle?"

"I want what you promised me."

"And what is that?"

"Sex so mind-blowing it'll make me forget who I am for a night."

Seems we're on the same page.

I pull her toward me while simultaneously spinning her around, making her back land flush with my front.

Delicately, I pull her long, silky hair to the side so that her neck is bared to me and plant a soft kiss just below her ear.

She lets out a muffled sound that sets my skin on fire, yet her entire body tenses.

"Relax, baby," I coax her, trailing another kiss down her neck. "You're safe with me." And another.

I drop soft kisses on her neck and massage her shoulders until she turns boneless under my touch, pliable.

I graze her nape with my teeth and trail my fingers along her spine until they reach the zipper of her dress. I pull it down an inch.

At once, her body tenses again against mine. Summer spins in my arms, her fingers lacing in the short hair at the back of my head. Her eyes shine with an unspoken need while her teeth keep her lower lip trapped as if to prevent the request from escaping.

"Tell me what you need, baby."

She caresses the hair at my nape, sending a shiver down my spine.

"I want you to kiss me first."

I push her two steps backward to the rear of the room until her shoulders hit the wall. I plant one palm on the wallpaper next to her face and use my other hand to tilt her chin up.

Her lips part and she sucks in a sharp intake of air.

The sound sets me wild. I drop my mouth to hers, and her lips part eagerly for me.

For someone who claims she doesn't like beards, she sure is kissing mine enthusiastically.

"Are you sure you're not into beards?" I tease as I pull back.

"You talk too much," she protests.

She presses against me to continue the kiss but I hold my distance, enjoying seeing Miss Prim so worked up.

Her lips are parted, and her eyes are heavy with desire.

"Archie," she whispers. "Please."

Hearing her whisper my name drives me insane. I capture her lips with mine, pressing her harder into the wall. I try to push a knee between her legs to get closer to her but her tight skirt is in the way. My hands trail down her sides to the hem of her dress, and I let my fingers play with the bare skin there. Slowly, I lift the fabric up. She lets me. Summer allows me to lift it up almost to her waist. Now I can wedge my thigh between hers, and I do. Then, without warning, I hook my hand behind her knee and lift her leg up, wrapping it around my waist.

She bites my lower lip in response.

I draw back, surprised. Summer is looking at me in a way that is shy and bold at the same time. This woman is so full of delightful contradictions.

"You can take my dress off now," she murmurs.

My blood sizzles in response to the challenge. Acting not so gentle anymore, I let go of her leg and flip her again so that her front is now pressed to the wall. I grab her arms and pull them up, placing her palms flat next to her face.

A pause lets me enjoy her labored breathing, then I pull the zipper of her dress down. It goes all the way to the back split of her skirt and pulls apart with a soft click. Her dress opens up like a reverse kimono, revealing pastel, lacy underwear that easily sheds a few years off my life.

I trail a knuckle down her spine, vertebra by vertebra. Kiss her neck again, her shoulder blades, her nape. Summer's breath comes in ragged gasps as I trace patterns on her skin with my tongue, easing her dress down as I go.

Her fingers clench at the wall as the dress pools around her ankles, leaving her in nothing but that lacy lingerie.

I can't control myself any longer. I need to have her now. I stand back. "You're going to kill me."

Her eyes cut to mine over her shoulder. And those dark pools of desire take the rest of my breath away.

That's it. I scoop her up into my arms and carry her to the bed. As I lay her down on the mattress, her hair splays out around her like a golden halo. Her chest heaves with each ragged breath. And she's so damn beautiful it hurts.

I take off my T-shirt, letting her gaze at my chest, and then lean over her. She grabs me by the shoulders, pulling me in for another kiss. Her nails sink into my skin; *now we're talking.*

"Please," she says again.

With inhuman effort, I pull up on my elbows, lifting away from her. Locking eyes with her, I say, "You can still change your mind; are you sure this is what you want?"

Our eyes hold, and I can see the vulnerability in hers.

"Don't make me beg," she whispers.

Summer arches into me and that's all it takes. Now I couldn't stop even if I wanted to.

7

SUMMER

Sunlight filters through the blinds, waking me up. I stir and stretch under the covers, not opening my eyes yet. I feel simultaneously rested and exhausted.

I blink. I don't recognize my surroundings. Honestly, I'm not sure when, where, or who I am. I turn my head and find two piercingly ice-blue eyes peering down at me.

Archie's lips part in a wicked grin. "Took you a minute there, didn't it?"

I can't help but smile back. Yeah, the man is cocky, but not without good reason. He made me forget my name for a minute after all.

Memories from last night invade my brain all at once. The sensation of his velvet-soft lips exploring my body and his beard deliciously tickling my skin. The way his chest felt pressed over mine. How he touched me like I was a precious thing but with an animalistic hunger at the same time that made me ache for more. Or the way he whispered dirty nothings in my ear as he brought me to heights of gratification I didn't even know existed.

Who knew sex with no strings could be this... liberating, explosive, exhilarating, and intensely satisfying. I should feel ashamed that I've leaned even more into the scarlet woman stereotype by jumping into bed with a man I don't even know. But I don't care. We're not hurting anyone, so it isn't anybody's business what we do. And it felt too good anyway. Even now I can feel an aftershock of pleasure coursing through my veins with just the remembrance of it all. Still, I'm not about to inflate his already large ego.

I straighten up on the bed, pulling the sheets along with me—not that there's any need for modesty at this point. A few more highlights of the night's activities quickly flash through my head, threatening to make me blush. So, I blink the memories away and address Mr. Cocky instead. "You don't do humble, do you?"

He raises his hands behind his head, elbows opened wide, biceps showing. "Never saw the point. Never had a reason to."

He throws me a side look that's enough to make my toes curl.

I need a break from all the testosterone.

"I need a shower," I say, trying to figure out a way to get out from under the covers without him seeing me naked. Ridiculous, I know.

"Want company?" Archie offers. "I'm the best at soaping up."

"No doubt," I say sincerely. "But I prefer to use my own room."

"Sure," he says with half a shrug, pointedly staring at me as if he knows I'm embarrassed to get up while he's looking.

But you know what, Mr. Cocky? If I'm not exactly bold by nature, I can sure fake it till I make it, especially when someone prods my pride. Acting carefree, I throw the sheets away from my body and hop off the bed, taking my time to retrieve my clothes from wherever we tossed them around the room. It's a reverse striptease. But it works just fine. Archie's eyes never leave my skin, I can tell even when I'm giving him my back. I turn as I pull the zipper of my little black dress up, and his hungry expression tells me I'm going to pay for the improvised performance next time he gets his hands on me. Ah, well, two can play this game.

My final act is to move out to the patio to retrieve my shoes. I pull one on and lean against the French windows, standing halfway inside the room to pull on the other.

"One last thing," I say, straightening up and smoothing the creases of my skirt down. "No one can know about our... arrangement. Especially not my sister."

I might not have done anything wrong, but I sure don't need the added gossip.

"I won't tell if you don't."

"Okay, but in public, we have to act as if we don't know each other. Like, at all."

Archie leans forward on the bed, the sheets rolling to the side and showing more distracting skin than I care to deal with right now. It's hard to keep my tone stern when so many muscles are on display.

"I can manage that," he says.

"Very well." I give my pencil skirt one last straightening shimmy and head for the door. "See you later."

I exit and close the door behind me, leaning my back against it for a moment. I let out a long exhale. Acting cool is exhausting. My heart is beating so fast I could've just come back from a—Aargh!

The door supporting my weight opens unexpectedly, and I tumble to the floor, landing on the carpet like a sprawled starfish. Above me, Archie is doing his best not to laugh while he peers down at me. My only consolation is that he's pulled on his boxer shorts before coming to the door. I wouldn't have cared for the fresh perspective on his... mmm... *Pickle? Willy? Banana?*

Oh gosh, and now he knows I'm thinking about his... *Princess Sofia?*

"You forgot your purse." He dangles the black clutch above me and offers me a hand to stand up.

I make a point of getting up on my own. Then, having forever lost all my coolness, I quickly grab my bag, nod an embarrassed thank you, and make a run for it.

* * *

Back in the safety of my room, I contemplate taking a cold shower. I sure could use one. But who ever enjoyed a cold shower? Do people really take voluntary ones? I don't think so. And my muscles are too sore from last night anyway to put them through a freeze fest. Honestly, I should skip the shower altogether and go for a bath—but there's not enough time for that, not if I want to catch the 8 a.m. yoga class I saw on the resort's activities schedule. I need the stretching, and to practice some guided relaxation techniques.

I compromise with a short but scorching hot shower. As searing hot as the memories from last night that keep assailing me. Archibald Hill has easily been the best sex of my life. True, I haven't had that many partners, but my ex, Robert, had years to get to know my body. What I liked and what I didn't. And Archie, in a single night, managed to blow even that out the window. And the worst of it isn't even the sex itself, but the way he made me feel. Like I was the only woman in the world, like nothing else mattered but us two tangled up in the sheets.

For someone who doesn't do love, Archie sure gives intense, looking-into-your-very-soul eye contact in bed. I turn off the tap and shake the thought away.

Quick, introspective shower over, I change into black leggings and a neon pink tank top ready to relax and try to forget the hitch last night has put deep down in my belly.

In the lobby, I follow the signs to the detached cabana where the class will be held. When I reach it, I'm ten minutes early and only the teacher— a medium-height, super-lean brunette in a ponytail—is here. To keep busy, I grab a yoga mat, position it to the far-left side of the giant thatched hut with sliding glass walls that are now closed, and enjoy the view of the vineyard while I stretch my thighs.

I'm balancing on my left leg, holding my right foot close to my butt with one hand in a standing quad stretch, when a warm breath brushes against my neck.

"Morning," Archie says.

And all I can say for myself is that I manage not to tumble at this man's feet for the second time in less than an hour. I narrow my eyes at him and follow his movements as he grabs a yoga mat and places it next to mine.

"Are you stalking me now?" I hiss. "I said no contact during the day."

He shrugs nonchalantly. "Just here for the yoga, honey." And then, leaning in closer so that only I can hear, he adds, "Do you think I could hold some of the positions from last night without regular training?"

My entire body flames up at the comment, but I'm spared the need to come up with a smart retort by the arrival of other hotel guests. I just scowl at him in a back-off way and step on my mat, pointedly staring forward.

Not a very long-sighted strategy. I should've moved to the other side of the cabana. Because from here, I'm either facing his well-rounded buns that even yoga pants can't hide or am all too aware he's turned toward *my* rear end. And as someone once said, leggings never lie. No matter that mine are the super covering type; I feel naked.

I know I'm being ridiculous because he's already seen me properly naked, but that doesn't stop me from feeling self-conscious. I try to focus on the teacher's voice, controlling my breathing, inhaling deeply through my nose and exhaling slowly through my mouth, and let the tension seep out of my muscles, but every time I glance over at Archie, he's grinning at me like the cat that got the cream.

Ah! So much for an hour of meditation and relaxation. Yoga is stressing me out more than having to talk to the dude. I should've taken a bath; that's where I should be right now, soaked to the neck in hot, bubbly water. Instead, I'm stuck two feet away from the very man I was trying to wash out of my system.

I'm so on edge that I don't immediately grasp what the teacher—Miranda—is saying. I automatically nod like the rest of the class, not knowing what I'm agreeing to. Must be something good if everyone else is on board.

"Very well," our instructor says, smiling at us. "Let's all pair off." She wiggles a finger between Archie and me.

Oh gosh, what did I say yes to? This is about to turn into the yoga session from hell.

"As I was saying," Miranda continues. "Acro Yoga is not a discipline for everybody, but I practice it often and teach it as well, and it has helped me detox a little from our lives spent holding devices. Acro is as much about the physical and platonic touch. It's a group activity that builds a sense of community, as we have to hold hands with strangers and trust them. In short, I love it, and I always try to promote its practice and encourage my students to try it out." Miranda smiles enthusiastically. "But beware, it can be addictive. Ready?"

The class yells a widespread, "Yeah!"

"Let's do it." She claps her hands once. "Today, I'll walk you through a few basic exercises that I hope won't be too challenging for anyone." She gives us another encouraging smile. "So, let's start with the very basics. To practice Acro Yoga, you need one person to play the role of base and one to be the flyer. Usually, the stronger, heavier person is the base."

Archie and I stare at each other, silently agreeing he's going to be the base.

"I'll circle to correct your posture and to make sure everyone's safe," Miranda carries on. "We're going to start our beginners' sequence with a plank on plank pose to help build core strength and learn how to support a partner. If you're the base, take plank pose with your hands shoulder-width apart, arms straight, core engaged."

Everyone designated as the base—all the men in the class and two women, we're five couples in total—assume the position.

"Very well," Miranda says. "Now, flyers, facing your base's feet, place your hands on their ankles, press down with straight arms, and place your left foot on their distant shoulder. Once you feel secure, place your other foot on their near shoulder and hold steady."

I grab Archie's ankles and follow the instructions. This isn't too bad; I'm looking at his heels and he's looking at the floor. The touch of my hands on his ankles is still a bit electrified. But there isn't much contact, platonic *or* physical.

So far, so good.

After thirty seconds—more than enough in plank—Miranda calls the pose off. "Okay, class, that was fantastic. Now let's try another pose that's amazing to build trust between partners, and to teach the bases how to support their flyers. This one's called plank press. Bases, please lie on your backs facing your flyers, knees bent, feet flat on the ground."

Archie turns on the mat and lies down, looking up at me. He's keeping a straight face, but his eyes are filled with mischief. I take a deep breath and wait for the rest of the instructions. I fear this pose won't be as easy-peasy lemon squeezy.

"Flyers, place your feet in between your partner's. Perfect." The instructor takes a quick look around the class and motions for me to advance a little. "Don't be afraid to really get in there."

I take another step forward, and Archie winks at me, causing a small butterfly explosion in my stomach.

"Now, bases," Miranda continues. "Set your feet hip-width apart on your flyers hips."

The contact is innocent but intimate. My hip bones are tingling. I didn't even know that was possible. And there he is with that intense eye contact again. He's not even touching me properly, yet I can feel the pressure of his feet through the thin layers of fabric on my leggings and it sends a wave of warmth throughout my body. If we were alone instead of in the middle of a group yoga session, by now I would've already leaned in and kissed him senseless. But we're not alone, and I can't lose focus.

Thankfully Archie doesn't move, mirroring Miranda's instructions for our mindfulness journey.

Being still helps.

The piercing light-blue eyes don't.

"Flyers, open your arms in a T shape and keep your bodies straight while maintaining a strong core. Bases, bend your knees toward your chest and receive your flyer's weight and then push back slowly. Flyers, plant your feet on the floor and trust your weight to the base. Try several times, each time coming in deeper."

Archie's lips curl at the corners, and his eyes burn into mine. Has yoga always been riddled with double entendres, or is it just this man that can make everything seem dirty, hot, sexual, and why aren't we in his bed right now? Maybe having morning sex is how I should've started the day, because this sure as hell seems like an extended foreplay session and I've no idea how long I'll have to wait before my next Archie fix.

Oh, gosh, what is wrong with me? One night with the guy and I'm already talking like an addict. Why can't I just be with a man and not care? Alarm bells sound in my head but I drive them away. I don't care about him. It's just the great physical connection we experienced last night after a year without a man's touch that's throwing me off. It'll wear off once I get my fill, right?

"Fantastic, class." Miranda claps, distracting me from my reverie. "Let's try out one last pose."

Thank goodness this will be over soon.

"This one is called the base test. And it's a very beneficial pose to help the base practice staying stable while the flyer lifts off. We're all good so far?"

The class cheers with varying levels of enthusiasm, prompting Miranda to keep going.

"Great. So, bases. Stay on your backs and lift your legs ninety degrees in an L shape, stacking your feet over your hips for stability." She waits for everyone on the floor to comply with the instructions, and then continues, "Now, flyers. Cross your forearms and settle your elbows in the middle of your partner's soles."

Once we're all in position, Miranda delivers the final stroke. "Now, make eye contact with your base to establish trust."

I lower my gaze to Archie's face, and a wave of heat slams into me. This is ridiculous. We've had sex, for heaven's sake. And this pose is chaste in comparison to what we did last night. But the eye contact is intense. His eyes are so blue, so penetrating. I feel like they can read my soul's deepest secrets.

Last night, in the dark, when his gaze became too intense, I could close my eyes and forget where I was and who I was with. Get lost in the physical aspect of it. Enjoy the moment without thinking of the consequences. Just feel good for once, without guilt, without regret, without worrying about what comes next. But this morning, the universe is forcing me to confront all my bad decisions.

No, "bad" isn't the right word. "*Dangerous*" is.

A light touch on my elbow distracts me. "Are you having trouble with the pose?" Miranda asks.

"No, why?" I turn to her, then look around the cabana. Everyone else has lifted off the floor and is perched on their partners' legs like parrots. But I got so lost staring into Archie's eyes, I didn't even hear Miranda utter the next round of instructions. "Sorry," I say. "I was just—"

"No need to apologize," Miranda interrupts me. "Take all the time you need. Whenever you're ready, fold your arms into your base's feet and slowly lift off the ground."

I nod and assume the pose. Then make the mistake of looking at

Archie again. No wink this time, but that doesn't save me from having butterflies exploding in my belly all over again.

How long do we have to stay in this position?

As if on cue, Miranda answers my prayers. "And, flyers, please slide back to the floor. Wonderful job, class, we've earned a few minutes of relaxation in corpse pose, yeah?"

I flee to the safety of my mat, lie down, and close my eyes, ready to disappear into a quiet spot in my mind with no Archibald Hills in it.

Easier said than done.

I try to follow Miranda's meditating instructions, but every fiber of my body is still hyper-aware of the man lying beside me. No amount of closing my eyes, opening my mind, letting my breath occur naturally, and allowing my body to feel heavy on the ground works.

Instead, my body feels light like a feather and... tingly.

"Work from the soles of your feet up to the crown of your head," Miranda says. "Consciously release every body part, organ, and cell."

Ah. All I can think about is how Archie's hands followed the same path last night, starting literally from the soles of my feet to end up tangled in my hair.

"Relax your face. Let your eyes drop deep into their sockets. Invite peace and silence into your mind, body, and soul."

Peace and silence, huh? I fear I've invited the *devil* into my mind, body, and soul.

8

ARCHIE

"Okay, class, it's now time to come out of Savasana." The yoga instructor's voice makes me jump alert.

With barely two hours of sleep under my belt, I was already dozing off. I hope I wasn't snoring.

"To exit the pose..." Miranda's soothing voice keeps rolling instructions I don't want to follow. All I want to do is curl up on my side and sleep. "Deepen your breath. Inhale and exhale. In through your nose, out through your mouth. Wonderful." She leaves us a few instants to breathe before continuing. "Now, bring gentle movement and awareness back to your body; you can start by wiggling your fingers and toes. When you're ready, roll to your side. Rest for a moment before slowly pressing into a comfortable sitting position. Inhale as you unfold your body, letting your head be the last thing to come into place. And exhale."

Once we're all up and ready to go, Miranda bows and says, "Try to carry the peace and stillness of Savasana with you throughout the rest of your day. I hope I'll see you all tomorrow."

The class bows in return, most looking relaxed. Not Summer. She's still on the pissy side. She's been glaring at me the entire time we've been doing practice together. The scowls mixed with copious blushing.

The woman is such a mystery. Last night, she surprised me by coming to my room. Heck, after her first response at the bar I thought I'd blown it, but not thirty minutes later and she was knocking on my door to give me one of the wildest nights of my life. The whole experience was surprising, to say the least. The way our bodies seemed to just fit together, the explosive chemistry between us, the way I couldn't stop looking into her eyes as we moved together. The way I *didn't* want to stop looking at her.

Which is... ah... something I shouldn't think about while wearing yoga pants.

Right. I meet Summer's evil eye and smile. With her skintight leggings, the high ponytail, and mixed-signal dirty looks, she has enough of a prim-but-shy cheerleader vibe to make me want to carry her back to my bed and sex the attitude out of her.

Something else I shouldn't think about while wearing yoga pants.

Speaking of dos and don'ts, she also said we should act like total strangers during the day. But I know women: what they say and what they mean are not necessarily the same. For example, "Pretend you don't know me" would probably translate to, "You can't just ignore me. Be nice and acknowledge we had sex, that it was fantastic, and that you can't wait to do it again, but do it in such a way no one but me will notice."

Easy, right?

So, before hitting the breakfast buffet, I act as any decent yoga partner would: I walk two steps toward her, nod, and say, "Great practice." I throw in a quick hug and a wink.

Chill enough that no one would suspect. But also intimate and conspiratorial enough, she knows I'm not ignoring her or acting like a douche or pretending last night didn't happen.

Perfect.

Still, Summer has gone all stiff on me and is glaring harder than ever. Her taut lips open only to mutter a strained, "See you around." And then she's off walking toward the resort, leaving me with a nice view of her indignant behind strolling away. Aaand... strike three on things I shouldn't think about while wearing yoga pants.

Ah, the woman is a real riddle. I thought we'd broken the ice last night, hell, melted a whole glacier. First with her opening up to me about her past, and then with the mind-bending sex that followed.

But it looks like I still have some work cut out for me. And where would the fun be otherwise? I've always enjoyed a challenge. But not on an empty stomach, as a loud grumble kindly reminds me. Ready to hit that buffet, I hop off the three wooden steps of the cabana and head inside.

The breakfast hall is wide and airy; the far-back wall is entirely made of floor-to-ceiling windows and overlooks the vineyards. In the morning light, the view is stunning. Orderly rows of vines stretch beyond the horizon and disappear behind a hill to reappear over the next crest. Roses blossom at the head of each row. And the sky is a glorious blue without a cloud in sight.

Someone shoulder-bumps into me. "Nice, huh?"

I turn to find my best friend and groom extraordinaire standing next to me, a plate filled to the brim with French toast in one hand and a cup of coffee in the other. Logan is rocking the nerdy-but-hot professor look: messy dark hair, green eyes hidden behind black-rimmed computer glasses he doesn't need but insists on wearing when not on a trip, a white dress shirt, and chinos. If this weren't his wedding, he'd be a great wingman, as he's proved on many past occasions. Good thing I'm already all set in the women's department for the week.

"Logie Bear." I give him a friendly slap on the shoulder.

He eyes me suspiciously. "Are you coming wine tasting dressed like this?"

Ah, yes, I'd forgotten about the week of meticulously planned *"fun"* the wedding party is supposed to have.

"No worries, man. I'll grab a quick breakfast and then I'll go get changed."

"Why don't you join me and Winter? We snatched a window table and there's still room."

"Great, let me get some food first and I'll be right there."

In a corner of the room, long, rectangular wooden tables covered by white cloths offer a vast assortment of breakfast treats both sweet and savory. I keep it simple and opt for a classic, piling a plate with blueberry pancakes. To complete the meal, I order a cappuccino at the bar and go join Winter and Logan at their table.

The soon-to-be Mrs. Spencer salutes me with a scowl frighteningly similar to that of her twin, even if the differences between the two sisters couldn't be more staggering. A short but intense acquaintance with Summer and a long friendship with Winter make me enough of an expert to pick them apart with my eyes blindfolded.

Winter is all about casual clothes, messy curls, and chewed-up nails. Whereas Summer keeps her hair straightened to death, is primpy to the bone even while wearing gym sweats, and has perfectly manicured nails. I shiver as I feel the phantom of their scratch running down my back.

Note to self: never wear yoga pants on this trip again. I quickly take the chair next to Winter to avoid a scandal.

"Oh, look who decided to show up," she greets me.

Guess I deserved this jab.

"Come on, Snowflake." I make doe-y eyes at her. "You know you can't stay mad at me."

The bride-to-be pouts.

"If you smile, I'll tell you about that time Logan and I went to Jordan."

"Man, not that story." Logan groans and gets up, saying, "I want some extra cinnamon; you guys need anything?"

We both shake our heads, so Logan goes.

Once he's a few steps away, I bat my lashes at Winter. "Are you still mad?"

She's about to crack, when Tucker joins the table, showing an even more pronounced sour-pussy attitude and ruining all my hard work in mollifying the bride-to-be.

"Good to see you aren't dead," he says in place of hello.

I study him. Curly brown hair, big brown eyes, trustworthy face. Dressed in a polo shirt and short cargo pants, he's the personification of a good boy. Guess he could do as a replacement wingman now that Logan is permanently out of the fray. We'll see.

"Guys, relax," I say, defending myself. "I missed *one* meeting, you don't need to get all touchy-feely on me."

"Easy for you to say," Winter mopes. "It's not *your* wedding."

"And"—Tucker piles more crap onto my plate—"you haven't spent several months planning it. Did you at least remember the rings?"

Barely.

"Of course, man, I wouldn't forget something so important. Listen, guys, yesterday I got held up in Berkley and I was late, but now"—I place my right hand over my heart and solemnly raise the other to take a sacred oath—"I'm here, 100 per cent invested in this wedding and ready to perform my best-man duties."

Tucker sits at the table, giving me a skeptically raised eyebrow, but Winter is working hard at suppressing a smile.

"All right, Golden Boy," she says. "You get a pass, but no more screw-ups."

Duly chastised, I nod, hoping getting naked with the bride's sister won't count as a screw-up.

Speaking of the devil. An image of naked, panting Summer appears before my eyes just as the lady materializes in the flesh behind me.

I know because Winter is waving and calling her over to our table, and even though I can't see her, I can almost picture Summer spotting me, furiously trying to come up with an excuse not to join her sister's table, failing, and coming over looking irresistibly pissy.

"Hey." Summer joins our group.

She takes the last free chair next to Tucker and does her best to avoid meeting my eye as she picks up a muffin, looking as subtly on edge as I predicted.

"Everything okay with you?" Winter asks.

"Yes, why? I'm cool; why wouldn't I be cool?" Summer replies in a slightly too-shrill voice that sounds all *but* cool.

Winter raises her brows. "You just seem a little keyed up."

"I'm just a little nervous about seeing everyone."

Winter throws her sister a regretful stare and lets the topic drop.

"Hey, Summer," Tucker says back.

"Hi, *Summer*," I echo, infusing the perfect amount of charm into the greeting. And then, just because, I decide to rock her boat a little. "Good to see you again so soon."

Winter stares back and forth between us. "You two know each other?"

The question prompts Summer to almost choke on the mini muffin she was eating, making her splutter and cough all over the place, her face

turning beetroot red. It remains to be seen if it's from the lack of oxygen or
from embarrassment. Gosh, the woman is terrible at keeping her cool
under pressure. She really doesn't come across as the had-a-months-long-
affair-with-my-best-friend's-boyfriend type.

To put her out of her misery, I say, "We were just partnered up in yoga
class." Then, turning to Winter, I add, "Hard to miss the resemblance."

Winter narrows her eyes at me and leans forward on her elbows. "Yo,
Golden Boy, dial down the charm a notch, won't you? My sister is off
limits."

Oops.

Guess this answers my earlier question.

"Hey," I self-deprecate a little. "I'm sure your sister has better things to
do than mingle with the likes of me."

I give Summer a mischievous wink, and she stares daggers back at me
while pretending to sip her latte.

"No, you're right," Winter says. "My sister isn't looking for a relationship right now."

"Oh, is that the case?" I ask.

This is so much fun.

"Yes," Winter replies. "Sammy has sworn off men for a while."

"Has she?" I ask. "And how's that working out for you, *Sammy?*"

And if looks could kill...

Summer's lips part in a kill-them-with-kindness smile so viciously
polite it lets me know just how much dirt I'll have to eat later. "Best decision of my life," she says.

That's when Logan rejoins the table, asking, "What did I miss?"

And I'd pay gold to know what everyone is thinking. Winter is clueless
about the tension between me and her sister. Tucker is looking at me
funny; he may suspect something. And Summer is turning my insides out
with the fierceness of her blue glare. I can't wait to have some angry sex
with her later. Today I'm in the mood for a little *bite.*

"I was about to tell the Jordan story," I say, finally cutting Summer a
break.

"Do you really have to?" Logan protests. "I still cringe every time I
think about it."

"What did you guys do?" Winter asks.

After an imperceptible "you're welcome I got you off the hook" nod at Summer, I launch into my narration. "Let me set the mood first. Imagine the sun setting on a scorching day while two lone figures come back from the desert. Rid of their mounts, they walk the city on foot. The men are sweaty, dusty, and, frankly, in need of a good shower. But also famished."

"You can stop speaking in the third person," Winter says.

"Okay, Snowflake, but you're ruining my storytelling mojo," I say, and resume my narration, switching to first person. "End of the day, we were dirty and exhausted, but even hungrier, so at the first open-air restaurant we saw on the way back to the hotel, we forfeited personal hygiene in favor of a good meal and sat at a table."

Logan puts a hand over his eyes and shakes his head.

"Problem was," I continue, "our Arabic wasn't up to par, and neither was the servers' English at this particular establishment. Our only option left to order was to point at other people's plates and, what do you know, it worked. They brought us food and water, and only then we noticed there wasn't any cutlery on the table. We tried asking a server with various degrees of gesticulating, but it became the dude's turn to point at the other patrons of the restaurant, who were all eating with their hands. Okay, we said, now convinced we were at some kind of super traditional restaurant, and ate with our hands. The dish turned out to be delicious, a mysterious mix of meat and rice and spices and whatnot. When we finished our portion, they brought us more, and not just once but twice. At this point, Logan and I began to wonder if we hadn't fallen victim to a scam and how much the bill was going to be. But, as per the language barrier, we had no way of explaining we were full. So, we sat and finished everything they brought us, down to the final dessert and tea."

Logan scoffs. "The cake should've been our clue, man."

"Why?" Winter asks, looking between me and her husband-to-be. "What happened?"

"In a minute," I say. "We finished eating and asked for the bill, of course without success. To make the server understand, I took a wad of cash out of my wallet and waved it in his face. My gosh, the humiliation." I pass a hand over my face. "The waiter stubbornly refused to take my money. I was about to get up and forcibly stick the bills in his pocket when the music started and, tah-dah... the bride and groom walked to the center of the stage and began to dance..." I pause a moment for suspense. "And that's how Logan and I accidentally crashed a Jordanian wedding, ate traditional *mansaf* with our hands, and lived another day to tell the tale."

Everyone around the table chuckles. Even Summer's lips are curled up in a hint of a smile that positively disappears when I wink at her.

* * *

The breakfast party breaks up soon afterward. Summer escapes to her room the moment she's taken her last bite of toast, claiming she has to go get changed. Winter and Logan are already dressed for the day, so they spend more time enjoying their coffee and the view while Tucker and I leave a few minutes after Summer. Our rooms are adjoining, so we walk together through the reception toward the elevators. We're about to get in when a tall, slender woman with light-brown skin, a halo of curls, and striking aquamarine eyes calls after us. "Excuse me? Are you the wedding planner for the Spencer Knowles wedding?"

Tucker sighs. "I'm not a wedding planner; I work logistics, and okay, I'm good with checklists and in-depth planning, stocking, organizing... but I never asked for this job. And I can't remember how they roped me into it, but now I'm stuck having to organize themes, color schemes, frocks, seating arrangements..."

"Fair enough," the gorgeous lady says... and if I didn't have my hands already full for the week, I'd probably choose this moment to make a brilliant comment and woo the missus. Instead, I keep quiet as she continues. "But you did plan *this* wedding, right?" And before Tucker can reply, she raises her hands, adding, "And before you tell me your entire life story again, this is a simple yes or no question."

Tucker pouts. "Yeah, I'm planning *this* wedding."

"There you go." Feisty Curls smiles. "I'm Christian Slade's PA. I'm sure you're aware he's on the guest list and will be in attendance over the weekend."

"Yes." Tucker grits his teeth. "I can read an RSVP card, thanks."

"Good for you." Her smile widens. "Anyway, I need to review a few security adjustments with you."

The elevator dings open behind us, and Tucker takes a step back inside. "Well, next time you need someone's help, I suggest you try not to be rude to them."

My friend gestures for me to come into the elevator. I do and am as surprised as Feisty Curls when he pushes the button to our floor without another word.

The woman is too stunned by his reaction to block the closing doors, but we can still hear her protests as the elevator climbs up. "What? I wasn't rude! Hey, you can't just leave... We need to talk... Come back...!"

The rest of her recriminations are muffled as we get past the first floor.

I low-whistle to my friend. "Man, that was some attitude."

Tucker is universally acknowledged as the friendly, teddy bear type. I swear, in all our years of friendship I've never seen him react this way to anyone, no matter how nasty the person.

"Well, could you believe her? She drops some famous person's name and expects the entire world to fall at her feet. Not gonna happen."

"Good for you." I jokingly punch him in the shoulder. "Show her who's boss. And a word of advice, if I may?"

Tucker glares at my sarcasm.

"You should bed the lady; she's a hottie."

Tucker snorts. "Yeah, as if *that* is gonna happen after our sweet meet-cute. Can you believe she didn't even introduce herself? Just name-dropped her boss. Rude."

"Dude, I can't believe how much she has you worked up with a two-minute conversation." The elevator dings open to our floor. "You should explore that chemistry." I exit, giving a military salute. "See you downstairs in a bit."

We walk down the corridor to our respective doors.

"Don't be late," Tucker says, pausing on the threshold. "I'm keeping a fifteen-minute grace period, but then we leave."

Mock-grave, I nod and unlock my door. Tucker shakes his head and disappears inside his room.

After a quick shower, I stop in front of the closet mirror and feel a little girly as I debate how to dress to better impress another feisty lady. Is Summer the loose, light sweater kind or a fitted T-shirt lover?

Since I'm her first beard, I decide to make the fantasy complete for her and opt for a subtle lumberjack look: faded jeans slightly loose on the hips, boots, tight-fitting black T, and an unbuttoned flannel shirt.

Irresistible and ready to rock.

Pity the sight that awaits me downstairs couldn't be any less rock 'n' roll if it tried. Outside the main hotel entrance, a bus is parked with its engine running while small groups of wedding guests pile in. Okay, I guess I've suddenly turned eighty and am going on a trip with my fellow assisted living inmates. I'm half tempted to flip the bus the finger and take the bike; but, to be fair, we're going wine tasting, so maybe being chauffeured around—no matter how uncool the vehicle—has its merits.

A hand slaps me on the shoulder, followed by Tucker's voice. "Come on, buddy, let's hop in. We don't want to be late."

I follow him inside, craning my neck to check where Summer is and what she's doing, but all I can see is a glint of blonde hair at the rear end of the bus. The lady is doing her best not to look up, and I can't even tell how she's dressed. She's seated in an aisle seat, the window one left empty, a clear message that she wants to ride alone. Regretfully, I've no plausible excuse to disrupt that plan, or even pass by to say hello. When Tucker takes a window seat halfway down the bus, I don't have an excuse not to sit next to him.

The bus fills up quickly, a mixed group of personalities. The academics are easy to pick out, and not just because I know some of them from past expeditions. They're a distinctive bunch and mostly fit into the serious, bespectacled stereotype. Except for Giovanni, a young Italian archeologist who is the Yin to my Yang: dark hair, darker eyes, tanned skin— cool to the bone, interesting competition with the ladies. We had more than a few cases of overlapping interests in that department while Logan and I spent a month in Rome doing research for one of our trips.

"Giovanni," I greet him, half rising from my seat to grasp his hand in a brotherly handshake.

"Archibald, my friend. Long time no see, too long. We have so much catching up to do."

"Good thing we have a week of booze tasting ahead of us and nothing else to do."

However brief, our conversation causes a line to form behind Giovanni, a single file of people extending outside the bus. The woman waiting at his heels stares at us passively-aggressively enough to prompt Giovanni to move on.

"All right, man. I'll see you later."

The moment Giovanni moves toward the back of the bus, the joy of seeing an old friend is replaced by a prickling sense of unease. What if he tries to grab the free spot next to Summer? I take more time than necessary to sit, following my friend's progress. True to expectations, Giovanni pauses next to Summer, staring hopefully at the empty seat to her left, but she stubbornly refuses to acknowledge his presence, never raising her gaze from her phone. And Giovanni can only move forward.

With a sigh of relief, I settle back in my seat, proud of my ice queen. She sure has mastered the cold-shoulder treatment. I hope never to get on the wrong side of that attitude.

When almost every seat in the bus is occupied, the driver peeks back over his shoulder, asking no one in particular, "Are we good to go?"

Tucker stares at his watch, probably checking if the fifteen-minute grace period has expired, and yells, "Let's go."

The driver pushes a button to close the front doors, but before they lock, a scream comes from the yard, "Wait!"

The driver reopens the doors and Feisty Curls climbs in, panting as if she's just run a long distance.

Next to me, Tucker stiffens, while pointedly staring out the window.

Miss Feisty Curls takes a quick scan of the seating arrangements, ignoring the few empty seats remaining in the front to head our way.

She stops beside me. "Excuse me?"

I give her a thirty-two-teeth smile, mostly to rattle Tucker. "How can I be of assistance?"

"Would you mind sitting somewhere else? I have to talk to your friend."

"Sure, dear," I say, eagerly getting up.

I pretend to consider the empty spaces in the front and then the one free spot left in the back. Ahem. As if there was a question. I seize the opportunity and, with a few quick strides, I'm standing next to Summer, politely coughing.

She stares daggers at me.

"I'm sorry," I say with excruciating politeness. "I had to move seats. Would you mind if I sat here?"

"Sure," Summer hisses without moving.

The bus jerks forward and I sway, my hips thrusting dangerously close to her face. Summer's horrified gaze lands on my general crotch area, and then her eyes rise to meet mine in a swirl of blue fire while her cheeks color.

I shrug apologetically. "Should I climb over, or are you going to scoot?"

Summer snatches her bag. "I'll scoot," she says, sliding over to the window seat.

That's when I notice her shoes. She's dressed remarkably low-key in a white T-shirt and jeans, but the shoes are espadrille-like sandals with a high wedge and a lace-up tie in a floral print that she's wrapped around her ankles and secured in place with two pretty bows. Oh, gosh. Those bows are killing me. They're such a tease. I want to see her with nothing but the damn shoes on.

She looks up and catches me staring at her wedges. We both stare at them for a second, and I hope she's remembering when her feet were captive in my hands to do with them as I pleased...

Summer sighs and stares out the window... the same cute blush still adorning her cheeks. I'd pay a million in cash to know what she's thinking right now.

9

SUMMER

An entire week of this is going to kill me. Archie is just *staring* at my feet, for heaven's sake, and I'm breaking out in a heat rash.

And what's with the lumberjack look? Has he decided to play out every single bad-boy fantasy I've ever had? Yesterday, in the lobby, with his leather jacket and all-black get-up, he was a tough biker. This morning at yoga, he was Mr. Sporty McSweatPanty. And now this. What next?

A snapshot of his ripped abs pops into my head, and I'm ashamed to say the next guise I want to see him is *au naturel*. Last night, we were in the dark and I didn't get to admire his body in all its glory. At least, not with my eyes; my hands did a wonderful job—and, oh gosh, I must stop obsessing about it.

"What are you thinking about?" Archie whispers close to my ear, making me jump in my seat.

I turn to him, seething. "It's none of your business."

A half-smile tugs at his lips. "Oh, I think it is all of my business. You're blushing."

"I said none of *this* during the day," I hiss. "And that includes flirting."

"All right," Archie says. "I'll just sit here and be a good boy."

I roll my eyes. Even the way he said "good boy" implies the opposite. I forcibly move my gaze away from his mouth and pointedly stare out the window. He's rattling me. But I have to confess, having him by my side is a nice, comforting barrier between me and the rest of the world. We're seated in geeky land at the back of the bus, surrounded by a group of Logan's colleagues, who all appear very scholarly, except maybe for the tall guy with the Italian accent. But up front, I recognized a bunch of other people besides Susan and Daria. And today I'll have to face them all. No bathroom stalls to hide in. Getting on the bus first and stowing away among the professors only delayed the inevitable.

Unfortunately, the journey to the winery is short, no more than twenty minutes, and when the bus stops, I can't suppress a worried sigh from escaping my lips.

Archie doesn't miss a thing. "Nervous?" he asks.

"Mm-hm."

"Don't worry, I'm here. And if it all gets too much we can always grab a cab back to the hotel and finish our conversation from last night."

I surprise myself by saying, "Can't we do it right now?"

His eyes darken at the suggestion, but he shakes his head. "Sorry, that'd look a teensy bit suspicious, and I'm on strict instructions to keep undercover." He casually drops a hand on my forearm. "But if push comes to shove, we can feign a headache halfway through the visit."

"Both of us? Wouldn't it be even more suspicious?"

"Nah." Archie shrugs and gets up. We're the last ones left on the bus. "By that point, everybody will have been properly wined and they won't care anymore. Come on." He offers me a hand. "Let's do this."

He pulls me up and precedes me out.

When we get off the bus, everyone else is already assembled outside the winery. We're waiting in a paved open space with a circular fountain in the middle. The reception is to the left, and in front of us, a sloped-ceiling, squat building with a round arch in its center leads to the vine-yards. A tall, square tower on the left makes the entrance asymmetrical. Beyond the arch, green grass and endless rows of vines extend past the horizon.

We're a big group, thirty people, maybe more, mostly on the younger side. Winter has arranged for the parents and other middle-aged relatives to take part in the same visit, but later in the day. A small mercy, meaning I can at least avoid my meanest aunts a while longer. My best friend might've forgiven me, but her mom is a different story.

From the front, Lana catches my eye and waves. I smile and wave back but quickly look away. I'm still not 100 per cent comfortable around her—mostly because I'm still too ashamed of what I did. Plus, she's hanging out with the rest of my old group of friends, while I'm loitering way at the back, hiding behind all the professors who form a pretty smart human barrier. With this many people, maybe I can keep a buffer between me and Susan, Daria, and Martha and Hector, a couple who were another regular in our gang. But what if I can't?

The initial signs of a panic attack—sweaty palms and accelerated heartbeat—threaten to make me hyperventilate when Tucker comes out of the welcome center and gives me the best news of the day.

"All right, everyone," he calls. "Please gather around. There are too many of us to go in at once; we have to split into two smaller groups. Blue bracelets go first, while orange bracelets have to wait fifteen minutes. Please come up front to receive a bracelet."

Archie turns toward me. "I'll go get ours," he offers, and my knees wobble a little with relief. "Anyone we want to avoid?"

"Yeah," I say, pointing at Susan and Daria. "The woman in the coral dress with the brown bob, and her friend with the shoulder-length balayage."

Archie cute-frowns. "Am I supposed to know what a balayage is?"

"Ah, no. It means lighter hair tips and dark roots, she's the one in the white pants. They'll probably be in the same group as Lana. You've met her, right?"

Archie nods. "Gotcha."

While Archie is gone, the guy with the Italian accent oh-so casually walks up to me, saying, "Fine day, huh?" He jerks his chin up to the sunny sky.

The weather, really? Is this how he's going to start a conversation?

"Yeah, very nice," I respond, equally dully.

He moves on to the next obvious topic. "You're the bride's sister, right?"

"Yep."

I'm saved from his next boring conversational tidbit by Archie's return.

He comes our way, walking rather aggressively and staring the Italian dude down. I swear, if he were a peacock he'd have his tail all rounded out in a show of male dominance.

"Hey, Gio," he says. "The bracelets are being handed out at the reception; we're in the orange group. Logan is in the blue with his wife-to-be."

Gio takes the hint and makes himself scarce, saying, "I'll go get mine."

I turn on Archie and glare at him. "What are you doing?"

His chest de-puffs, and he shrugs innocently. "Nothing."

"The next time you do *nothing*, try to be less of a caveman about it. I told you no one can find out about us. And your little scene was completely unnecessary, anyway; your friend is the worst flirt ever."

"Really?" Archie scrunches his face, surprised. "Must be the Californian air, because in Rome, he used to make conquests left and right every time we went out."

"He spoke about the weather," I hiss.

"Ouch." Archie makes a mock-pained expression and then says, "Hold out your wrist."

I do, and he takes my arm in a gentle grip, his eyes burning with such passion he might be putting a wedding band on my ring finger. Of course, in Archie land, a ring would only mean: I promise to sex you up good, from now till the end of the week. Nothing remotely romantic.

Still, my pulse speeds up. And when he looks down at my wrist, I follow his gaze and have to work hard not to shiver while he fastens the orange bracelet around it. My skin burns where his fingers graze it, and why does this feel so much like foreplay? Can this man turn everything into a dirty thought, from foot massages to yoga classes to simple tour bracelets?

We can't be doing this in public. So, the moment the bracelet is secured, I snatch my hand away, croaking a coarse, "Thanks."

His gaze still consuming, Archie purrs back a, "You're welcome."

And his voice is alluring enough to send another shiver down my spine.

Thank goodness Tucker cuts into our covert seduction game, yelling, "All right, group one, those with a blue bracelet, please follow your guide inside."

Half the people trail under the arch behind a tall, blonde lady with a pixie cut. When they're gone, I do a quick scan of the remaining individuals, sighing in relief when I don't recognize anyone except for Italian Guy and Tucker, who joins our duo, saying, "Now I understand why teachers back in high school hated bringing us kids on field trips. This is exhausting."

Archie pats him on the shoulder. "You're doing a brilliant job, man!"

Before Tucker can reply, a tall, lean woman with light-brown skin, a crown of black curls, and striking blue-green eyes joins us, asking, "How smashed are we going to get?"

Tucker shrugs. "I don't know, how *smashed* can you get with four glasses of wine?"

The woman smiles. "On an empty stomach? Pretty damn smashed."

Then she looks up at Archie, taking in his ice-blue eyes, chiseled face, and devil-may-care grin and... is she blushing?

She extends her hand. "I don't believe we were properly introduced. I'm Penelope Jones."

And, okay, I'll admit that if I had feathers, now I'd be puffing them out while making scary, possessive squawking noises to intimidate a rival.

Archie shakes her hand with a noncommittal, "Archibald Hill."

Then the woman turns to me, her smile equally bright. "Penelope, but everyone calls me Penny."

I take her hand, my fighting instincts relaxing considerably. "Summer Knowles."

"You're the bride's sister," Penny says. "And sorry, everybody must make the same dull observation to you."

Despite my ridiculous jealousy of a moment ago, I like this woman. "Yeah, I am, and, yes, everyone does, but it's okay."

Penny returns her attention to Tucker. "How long before they bring out the booze?"

"The tour is supposed to last seventy-five minutes, so I guess at least half an hour to forty-five minutes will be taken up by the winery and cellar visit."

Penny grimaces. "What a bore."

Tucker bristles. "If you just wanted to drink wine, you could've gone to a bar."

Penny bristles right back. "No, I couldn't have. Since you couldn't spare five minutes to talk to me earlier, I had to chase you here."

"Next time ask nicely," Tucker says, and walks away toward a tall, portly man with white hair. Our tour guide, I presume.

The man claps his hands to attract everyone's attention and instructs us to follow him through the arch into the winery.

Penny skips ahead to follow him, while I hold back and lean into Archie. "What's their deal? Do they like each other?"

He shrugs. "Oh, definitely. I bet they're going to bang before the week is over."

I roll my eyes. "Romantic much, are we?"

Archie grabs my hand and pulls me forward. "Come on, let's go enjoy the tour."

But I yank my hand free, hissing, "No overt touching."

Archie throws me a devilish side-stare that promises retaliation. "If those are the rules."

* * *

Sweet torture is what he dishes out to me as a result, made of casual touches, brushes of skin on skin, and whispered words when no one's watching. By the end of the first half of the tour, I'm so turned on I'd gladly skip the wine tasting and go straight back to the hotel. But, of course, we can't.

The degustation room at least is air-conditioned; this way I won't have to fan myself when Archie unleashes his next move. The décor is similar to what I imagine a European monastery would look like. The ceiling is a vault of stone. Three of the four walls are made of the same material, while the front one is glass. In its middle, a door—also glass—opens onto a square courtyard.

The only furniture in the room is a rectangular wooden table that takes up the entire length of the space, chairs, a wine refrigerator, and a cabinet for glasses.

On the table, fifteen stations, each equipped with four empty glasses, have already been prepared. I sigh in relief that the two groups are being kept separate for the tasting part of the tour too. So far I've managed to avoid all of my all ex-friends.

The thought has barely left my mind when my other problem resurfaces. Archie oh-so casually brushes behind me, hands on my shoulders, with an apparently innocent "Excuse me," whispered into my ear.

At once, I feel like I'm pressed against the wall of his room again, with him turning me into a rag doll with no spine with his touch and kisses.

I grab a chair to sit down, hoping the wine will distract Archie long enough to end my torment.

Vain hope.

Archie immediately takes the seat next to me, pressing the side of his leg against mine.

And the torture starts anew.

Add wine into the mix, and by the time we're back on the bus and pulling into the hotel's parking lot, I unashamedly whisper in his ear, "Your room, fifteen minutes."

He smiles, making a pretend-offended face. "I thought we weren't doing *that* during the day."

I throw him a look that could kill. "Order some food; we can eat *afterward*."

As the bus stops, I wait for everyone to disembark and hopefully disperse before I exit myself. With a complicit nod, I shoo Archie away and follow him into the lobby two minutes later. Head low, eyes on the ground, I'm making a run for the elevators when my sister calls me.

I lift my gaze and search for her in the hall. She's with Logan near the reception area. I walk to where they are, plastering a smile on my face that I hope doesn't read: let's make this quick, I want to go have sex with the best man.

"Hey, you," my sister says. "I barely saw you all morning."

I lift my wrist, showing the orange bracelet. "Different groups."

"Did you enjoy the tour?"

I shift weight from one foot to the other. "Uh? Oh, yeah, great."

"Which was your favorite?"

"My favorite what?"

My sister blinks. "Wine?"

"Uh..." I honestly can't remember a single name or thing that was said about the vintages we tasted. So, I go with the only answer left to me, since we tried three reds and a white. "The white one, so refreshing."

Winter frowns. "Really?" She knows I prefer reds.

"Well, yes, for morning drinking on an empty stomach."

"Are you sure you're okay?"

Sweat pools underneath my armpits. Gosh, what's with the third degree? "Yeah, yeah, just a little lightheaded. You know what? I'm going to go take a nap; also need to pee really bad after drinking all that wine. See you later."

And before Winter can rope me into having lunch together or something, I turn on my heel and flee to the elevators.

I freshen up in my room and then move one floor up to Archie's.

Luckily, I don't run into anyone, neither in the elevator nor in the hall. I knock on his door and he opens it, still wearing the jeans and flannel shirt, all lumberjack hot. "You're late," he says.

Pushing him inside, I reply, "Then let's make up for lost time right away."

10

SUMMER

A few hours later, I reluctantly get out of Archie's bed to rush back to my room, shower again, and make myself presentable for dinner with my parents.

Logistics-wise, my family has kept the dinner arrangements simple and booked a table at the hotel. Not at the resort's fine dining restaurant, but at the pool-side grill bar. Tonight has turned out chillier than yesterday, so when I reach the grill bar, the hostess leads me to an indoor table overlooking the outdoor pool. Beyond the pool, hills covered in tidy rows of vines stretch to infinity. The view at sunset is breathtaking.

Both my parents and Winter and Logan are already seated at our table, so I'm the last one to join.

I check my watch: 7.29 p.m. Last, but not late.

With a preparatory sigh, I pull back the only empty wooden chair and sit between Winter and my dad.

"Hey, everyone," I say breezily.

The men at the table hum a noncommittal greeting while my mom X-rays me for a little longer than I'm comfortable with.

"Hi, honey, you look good," she says, as if surprised.

Since the affair was made public, she's been looking at me like she's wondering where she went wrong in my upbringing and why her usually better-behaved, perfect daughter suddenly turned into such a scandalous mess.

"Yeah," Winter joins in. "You're practically glowing. What's happened to you?"

So, I'm all sexed up, and it shows. Feeling more like a daredevil than usual, I reply with a half-truth. "I spent the afternoon in bed." I stretch my back like a still-sleepy cat. "I really needed it."

"Oh, well," my mother continues, "I haven't seen you looking this healthy since before the…" She lets the unfinished phrase hang in the air, positively crushing my good mood.

"Gosh, Mom, you resisted all of, what, five seconds before you had to mention the big scandal?"

"I was only trying to pay you a compliment."

"Yeah, sure."

I steal a side glance at Winter and notice my sister is approaching eye-rolling territory really fast. Right. This is her week, her wedding, and no matter how annoying my mother's habit of bringing up Johnathan within five minutes of seeing me is, I owe it to my twin to keep the tension at a minimum.

So, I turn to my dad and ask, "Did you guys enjoy the visit to the vineyard today? Amazing how fast they recovered after the huge fire of last year, huh?"

Out of the corner of my eye, I notice my mom shutting her mouth and swallowing whatever comment she was about to make, hopefully taking the hint that we all have to do our best to keep this dinner civil for Winter's sake and not mention the unmentionable.

I can't completely blame Mom for her attitude. In public, she's defended me like a lioness, telling everyone who cared to listen they had no business sticking their nose into my private life and that they were in no position to judge. She even fought with her best friend, Lana's mom, over The Mistake. But behind closed doors, it has been a very different tune since the magazine interview Johnathan the Bastard was paid to give went public.

My ex isn't famous, but Lana was already dating Christian at the time, and the paparazzi were out to get any specks of dirt they could on her past.

Johnathan was more than happy to oblige them. In the interview, he called our affair a mistake—hence how I named it from that moment on. He made me sound like a devil's temptress. But worst of all, he depicted Lana as a heartless gold digger who wouldn't forgive him now that she had a famous boyfriend. John spread all that suffering for a ten-thousand-dollar payday. As eye-openers go, mine was pretty devastating. I'd ruined my life, I'd hurt the kindest person in the world, and for what? For someone who cared more about getting a check than he did about me.

Since then, I've lost count of the times my mom has asked me, "Why?" or said, "Please, darling, help me understand."

As if it was that easy. I still can't process the particular brand of insanity that made me do the unspeakable. And I know Mom means well, but I'd rather not be reminded of The Mistake at every single family gathering for the next twenty years.

At least for tonight, my prayers get answered and, past the initial glitch, we manage to carry on polite conversation for the entire meal and steer clear of incendiary topics.

When everyone is done with their desserts, I search my bag for my phone, find it, and fire a quick text to Lana to check if she needs my help on anything for tomorrow—when we're having the bachelorette party.

TO LANA

Hey, you in your room? Can I stop by?

"Who are you texting?" Mom asks.

I lift my eyes from the screen, wanting to say, "None of your business." But as per my new This Is Winter's Week, Let's Not Ruin It policy, I go with, "Lana. I'm checking if she has everything sorted for tomorrow, or if she needs help with any last-minute details."

"Oh, what are you girls doing?"

I smile a little viciously, staring at the groom. "It's top secret; I can't divulge that information."

Logan groans. "If it involves male nudity, I'd prefer not to know."

My grin widens. "Sorry, pal, but the day is going to be filled with studs."

The professor shakes his head. "Now I really don't want to know."

I don't tell him the studs are actual horses, and that we've planned to spend most of the day at a riding ground.

My sister narrows her eyes at me. "I told you I didn't want a stripper."

"Hey, don't look at me," I snap. "I'm not in charge of the event; the maid of honor is."

Okay, that came out snarkier than I intended, bringing to the surface more touchy-feely emotions than I cared to reveal.

"Summer," Winter says, "I didn't pick Lana as maid of honor to punish you for what happened."

I shrug. "Whatever."

Now that the topic is out there, I can no longer pretend it didn't sting that my sister didn't ask me to be her maid of honor.

My phone pings with Lana's answer.

FROM LANA

Sure, come up whenever you want

I flip the screen toward the table. "Speaking of the devil," I say, getting up. "I'd better go before it gets too late." I nod at my parents. "Thank you for dinner." And then I wave at my sister. "See you tomorrow."

I don't wait for anyone's reply and practically flee the restaurant. I know I'm acting like an ass, but sometimes I really can't stand the way my family looks at me. I know I've let them down, that I went from perfect child to problem child in a blink, and that none of them will ever be able to look at me the same after what I did. But couldn't they let me forget it at least for an hour or two?

Yet maybe I don't deserve to forget, not even for a minute.

When I knock on Lana's door ten minutes later, I'm still rattled by the dinner and the dark thoughts it has stirred up.

"Hey." She opens the door with her usual warm smile, takes me in once, then does a double take.

Wow, do I look that horrible?

But she surprises me by saying, "You look great."

"Really?" I enter her room, and she shuts the door behind me. "Because I feel awful."

"Why? What happened?"

"I semi-argued with my mom at dinner about you-know-what." I plonk on a chair. "And then I got mad at my sister for picking you as maid of honor over me."

Lana sits on the bed opposite me. "Summer, you do know why she picked me, right?"

"Because I'm the undesirable twin number one?"

"No, because being maid of honor means you have to deal with a lot of the guests to organize stuff, and she didn't want you to be uncomfortable with... certain people?"

I hide my face in my hands. "Oh my gosh, I'm a total idiot. And I..." I stare up at my best friend, who I love to bits and don't deserve, and I can't help being overwhelmed once again by the enormity of what I did to her. Crap, I'm crying now. *Ugly* crying. A chest-shaking sobs and wailing fest.

Lana's eyes go wide. "Hey, what's up?" She gets up from the bed and crouches next to my chair.

"I'm sorry," I sob. I know I already apologized to Lana ages ago. That she's already forgiven me. But I feel like I need to say it again, even if words can never truly express the depth of my sorrow. "For everything I did to you. I'm so, so sorry. And I know nothing I'll ever do or say will make it right, but... I'm..."

"Sorry?" Lana offers with half a smile.

I nod. And I'm not sure who makes the first move, but suddenly we're standing and hugging while Lana pats my back, murmuring, "It's okay, everything is going to be okay."

I lean into her soothing touch for a while until I'm ready to let go. "You shouldn't be consoling me. Also, you're going to be a great mom one day."

Lana laughs it off, before asking, "Is that why you wanted to come over?"

"No." I blow my nose in a tissue. "I wanted to ask if we're all set for tomorrow, or if you needed help with any last-minute organizing?"

"No thanks. I had a lot of help from Tucker; we're good to go. That guy should plan weddings for a living, no matter how much he says he hates it. He's a natural."

"Okay." I dry my eyes on the back of my hands. "I'd better go apologize to my sister before she goes to sleep."

I pull Lana into another meaning-charged hug, whispering, "Thank you."

We say good night, and I wander back down to the first floor, ready for one more atoning pilgrimage.

I knock on my sister's door. When there's no answer after about a minute, I knock again harder, calling, "Winter? Are you in there?"

I hear rustling on the other side. A piece of furniture gets knocked over. A giggle. More shuffling. More giggles.

Winter opens the door wearing a white robe and looking positively flushed.

"Hi," she says, all pink cheeks and sparkly eyes. "What's up?"

"Hey, I'm sorry for snapping at you at dinner."

"Oh, that, phhf." She throws her hands down, palms to the ground, in a never-mind gesture. "Don't worry."

"But after Thailand, we agreed we'd never go to bed angry, so—" A door slams shut at the other end of the hall, distracting me. It's kind of awkward to have this conversation standing outside her room. "Hey, do you mind if I come in for a second?"

Winter stares at the floor. "Mmm, actually, this is not a good time."

When our eyes meet again, the penny drops, as does my jaw. "Oh my gosh, were you having sex?"

"No," she says, by which she means *not yet*. "Listen, we're good," she continues. "I'm sure Lana explained why I picked her to be the maid of honor, and it has nothing to do with me still being mad at you."

The fact that my sister basically knows how my conversation with Lana went without me needing to tell her is a testament to how symbiotic our trio is.

"Yeah, sorry it took her spelling it out for me to understand."

"Not at all. Are we cool?"

I nod.

"Great, good night."

In a blur, she pulls me into a hug, lets go, and, just as quickly, pushes me out of the way and shuts the door in my face.

Okay, then, the please-get-lost-and-let-me-have-sex-with-my-fiancé message is loud and clear.

And I can't wait for my own sex marathon to start, but I make one last stop before going back to my room. I knock on my parents' door and pull my mom in for a hug.

"Oh, honey." She hugs me back. "Do you want to come in and talk?"

"Honestly, Mom? No. I just wanted to let you know that I love you, and I'm sorry... for everything."

"I know, baby. And I know I can be a little smothering sometimes but it's only because I worry."

"I know, Mom. Sorry for snapping at you at dinner, but please try not to bring up the past so much, yeah?"

She nods and we hug again. I shoot a quick good night to Dad and, round of apologies over, I dash to my room. In the bathroom, I brush my teeth, take off my makeup, and change into comfy clothes. Finally, I'm ready to go to Archie's. I swear I've visited all the hotel's floors tonight. Winter and Logan's guests must occupy at least a third of the resort; it would've seemed logical to assign us an entire floor, but, no, we're scattered all over the place. Which, as annoying as it is, at least affords me some privacy.

By the time I knock on Archie's door, it's already late and I'm suppressing a yawn.

Archie answers the door, as impossibly attractive as ever: bearded, bare-chested, and ripped.

"Hi." I quickly scoot into the room before anyone sees me.

"Hey, how was dinner?"

I sag onto the bed like a dead weight. "Exhausting. I snapped at both my mom and my sister. Had a mini breakdown in Lana's room. Then I had to go apologize to everyone. Gosh, I wish Winter would get married tomorrow so I could go home and not see anybody for a month."

Archie sits next to me, a cocky eyebrow raised. "Should my pride be hurt?"

I smile up at him. "No, you're the only de-stressing factor in all this."

"Come here."

He pulls me between his legs, my back resting against his chest, and begins to massage my shoulders.

I moan. "Mmm, so you're not good only for foot rubs."

"I'm good for a lot of things," he whispers in my ear.

I close my eyes and relax into his embrace. He's so warm, and I feel safe in his arms. But I can't quite forget what happened earlier at dinner, or shove away the guilt gnawing away at my insides. It feels wrong to be even marginally happy when I know my family is still so edgy around me.

"Why did you fight with your mom *and* sister?"

"What do you think? The same old story."

I start to tell him what happened. When I finish, Archie simply pulls me closer and kisses my forehead. He doesn't offer any advice or platitudes; he just listens attentively and holds me like he understands that sometimes all one needs is for somebody to be present without judgment, without having to do anything else but be there by your side.

"How about you? How was your dinner?"

Archie chuckles. "I actually forgot to eat."

"What?" I turn around in his arms to face him. "How come?"

"Passed out right after you left and woke up only a while ago to shower."

"Are you hungry?"

The look he gives me back!

"For food I mean."

Archie brushes a stray hair out of my face. "Not really; I had a snack."

He presses his lips to my temple. Then he shifts and lies on the bed next to me. His arm pulls me closer while his other one tenderly cradles my head like a pillow on top of his chest as we talk about anything and nothing.

He tells me more stories from his travels, he makes me laugh—and it's enough to ease everything that was bothering me before: the guilt from earlier, my thoughts of never being good enough or pleasing anyone with what I do... They all seem so distant now.

I don't want this moment to end but soon, my eyelids grow heavy from exhaustion. I close them just a moment, listening to Archie's soothing voice, relishing the small circles he's trailing on my shoulders...

Next thing I know, I'm blinking awake and awash in sunlight.

Did I fall asleep on him? I must have. Archie's hands on me were so relaxing, his voice so soothing.

Now, in the cold light of day, we've switched positions and are spoon-ing. I remove his arm from around my waist and push up on an elbow, careful not to wake him.

I study his face. He looks serene, and, honestly, more beautiful than any man has a right to be. To have cheekbones like that, and with no contouring, it's not fair. And his best feature, those piercing blue eyes, is not even on display yet.

My heart beats to a weird thump, thump, thump frenzied tempo inside my chest. Somehow, sleeping together without *sleeping* together feels more intimate and dangerous than just having sex. What am I doing here? It hasn't been two days, and I'm already sort of relying on this man to be my rock. The person I confide in before going to sleep. A lumberjack in flannel armor who listens and doesn't judge, who manages to make me laugh even when I'm feeling overwhelmed by my mistakes. The man who gives me feet and back rubs when I'm stressed. But he's also the one who has told me in no uncertain terms that he's not interested in being anyone's rock, at least not in the long run.

The thought sends me into a slight panic. And when I panic, I run. Careful not to disturb him, I slip out of bed. But to sneak out of the room and let him wake up alone seems too much of a dick move. Instead, I move into the kitchenette and make a pot of coffee. I try to be as quiet as I can so that when I fill two paper cups and place one on the nightstand on Archie's side, he's still sleeping like a baby. I've no idea how he likes his coffee. Black? With milk? Full of sugar? The other day at breakfast, he was drinking a cappuccino, so maybe not black. I add a creamer pod and two bags of sugar next to the cup.

As a final touch, I find a notebook of hotel stationery and a pen and scribble a simple message:

See you at yoga, x

Once I'm back in my room, I call his. A coward's wakeup call, but necessary since I don't want Archie's coffee to go cold, or for him to sleep in and miss yoga. We're not going to see much of each other today. Which, in theory, is a good thing. No matter how much I'm dreading it, it's time I faced the world on my own two feet. But I still want to wish him good morning, in person. And yoga class is the perfect setting. With people around, we won't be able to discuss why we spent the night *just* cuddling, or why I fled his room this morning.

I let the line connect for three rings and hang up. That ought to do it.

11

ARCHIE

Stop. Make it stop.

A shrill noise is drilling a hole into my sleeping skull. I turn my face to the right, following the source of the earsplitting sound, and blink awake. My eyes focus on the now-silent room phone accusingly. Was it ringing or did I dream it?

It must've been ringing. Why else would I be awake? And why do I feel cold? I swear I spent the night wrapped in warmth and softness.

Next to the phone, I notice a paper coffee cup that I'm sure wasn't there last night. Underneath it, a note.

I touch my hand to the paper cup, still warm, and turn my head to the other side of the bed, empty. I feel the mattress. Also still warm.

I read the note:

See you at yoga, x

Ah.

What should I make of this? I wonder what made Summer freak out and leave before I woke up. But I also smile to myself realizing she's too nice to just sneak out, and made me coffee first.

Women.

The man who understands them is a lucky bastard, if the dude exists.

Conscious I'm not him and probably never will be, I shrug and sit up in bed, leaning against the headboard while sipping the coffee.

Mmm. Not too bad considering it came from a hotel kitchenette. Still, I grab the creamer Summer left on my nightstand, and mix it in. I close the plastic lid and take another sip; much better. Again, I smile to myself that she went to the trouble of leaving me the creamer and sugar. I still would've preferred a *bonjour* kiss, but as morning after cop-outs go, this isn't half bad.

Coffee over, I take a quick shower and change into yoga clothes, arriving at the class just as it is about to start.

Summer turns and spots me walking from the hotel to the outdoor cabana, her facial expression quickly switching from worried, to relieved, to a warm smile.

And I'm struck a little dumb in my tracks.

That is a smile that could launch a thousand ships, you know, if we were living in ancient Greece or something. A smile that could light up a whole town, and it's just for me.

A weird *something* wells up inside me. It's a warmth that I don't recognize and it startles me. It seems too serious. And right now, at this point in our relationship—if we even have one?—shouldn't we just be having fun? So why did I spend the night talking to the woman instead of making her scream my name between the sheets? And why did having her fall asleep in my arms feel just as good?

Summer lowers her gaze, pulling on her ponytail in a way that has me itching to reach out and pull down on her hair until her throat is exposed to me, until I can make her knees go weak with my mouth on her slender neck.

There goes the weird warmth surging in me again. I should run. I should turn on my heel and run as fast as I can. But I can't help it. I'm drawn to her in a way that's turned me into a fool. I act like a dumbstruck idiot half the time I'm around her. I don't even recognize myself.

Then Summer looks up and her smile turns flirty.

I stumble and almost fall face-first into the gravel, but luckily recover my balance with the next stride and manage to reach the cabana without making a complete ass of myself.

"Morning?" I say, underlining the greeting with a questioning tone: *"Are we okay?"*

"Morning." Summer nods in what I suppose to be a, *"Yep, we're good,"* unspoken answer.

Miranda, the same yoga teacher from yesterday, is confabulating with a small group of the other students in the class. She looks up, seemingly taking a headcount, and finally walks up front to the center of the space.

"Hello, class," she greets everyone. "I was just talking with a bunch of you who have expressed an interest in trying out more Acro Yoga poses. Since we're an even number again, I wanted to check if everyone would be okay with a slightly different class?"

I look at Summer. She shrugs, so I shrug right back.

"Everyone good with it?" Miranda asks, and when no one objects, she continues, "Great. We're going to do a quick warm-up and then work on some new poses."

A few sun salutations later, Miranda asks us to divide up into pairs. The same couples from yesterday form, and we wait for the next instruction.

"Okay," Miranda encourages, "for the next pose we're going to start with a position you're already familiar with but take it to the next level. We start in plank press. Bases, please lie on your backs facing your flyers, knees bent."

I get down on the mat and stare up at my partner. I love how Summer blushes whenever she meets my gaze and tries to hide it.

"Flyers, place your feet in between your partner's. Perfect. Now bases," Miranda continues. "Like yesterday, set your feet on your flyers hips."

I never thought of yoga as foreplay, but this Acro thingy sure feels like it.

"Let's practice a basic plank press a few times. Flyers, open up your arms in a T shape and keep your bodies straight and remember to keep a strong core. Bases, bend your knees toward your chest and receive your flyer's weight and then push back slowly. Flyers keep your feet on the floor and trust your weight to the base."

Take this move, I'm basically using Summer as a bench-press weight. It shouldn't feel hot. But it does. It's in the way she looks at me. In the way her ponytail swishes forward wherever I bend my knees, in the way her lips slightly part as if she was coming up for air.

"And now let's move on to the next level," Miranda says. "Flyers, reach forward and clasp hands with your bases, keeping your arms straight and creating a straight line from your shoulder to your bases. And now the hard part: flyers, you have to push off the ground. Bases, you have to lift your flyers, straightening your legs. Flyers, once you're airborne, engage your core and straighten your legs. If and when you feel stable enough in your balance, you can let go of your bases' hands and pull your arms back like bird wings in front bird pose."

Okay, this pose and the next ones require enough strength and concentration that I don't have much time left for dirty thoughts. Still, already compared to yesterday, Summer's and my movements seem to be much more fluid. Like we already have that extra confidence in each other. Is that why she bailed this morning? Was spending the night in each other's arms too much? And why? We agreed that this thing between us was a week-only deal. So, is she afraid we're getting too close? Is she getting too close? It wouldn't be the first time a woman I'd agreed to have a casual relationship with wanted more.

And, then, out of nowhere, the scariest thought I've ever had pops into my head: what if *I* wanted more?

The idea distracts me, making me lose concentration and causing my legs to wobble. Which, in turn, causes Summer to tumble down on top of me, her face landing ridiculously close to my groin. She stares up at me, shocked at first. Then, when she realizes where her pretty head is, her expression turns to embarrassment.

"Are you all right over there?" I ask.

Summer blushes and scrambles back, sitting on her heels.

Miranda comes next to us. "Is everyone okay?" she asks, and when we both nod, she adds, "It's perfectly normal to fall a few times when you're trying out these new poses for the first time. Class, I think we're done for today. How about a final stretch before I let you go have breakfast?"

Good, I think. A cool-down is exactly what I need right now.

Once the class is over, I almost expect Summer to walk off, leaving me behind as she did yesterday. But she lingers instead, and we walk together toward the breakfast room. To an outsider, our attitudes would come across as completely innocent, but, again, the shift compared to yesterday morning, when all Summer wanted to do was to shake me off, is incredible. Now she doesn't have a problem being at the croissants table at the same time as I am, brushing her shoulder against mine. At the coffee machine, she lets me lean into her from behind, my chest pressed to her back, as I reach for the creamer. Yesterday, she would've bolted like a startled deer.

We sit at the same table as yesterday, with the same companions. But again, Summer's stance couldn't be any more different. Instead of trying to avoid my gaze at all costs, she gives me flirty eyes from across the table for the whole meal.

It's the sweetest torture. Makes me want to skip the bachelor snooze fest—err... party—and bring her back to my room. She knows it, and she knows I can't, and she's messing with me, playing a little game of hide and seek.

We all get up to leave together, exiting the breakfast room and then lingering in the hotel's lobby. Tucker swears; he's forgotten his phone at the table and goes back to pick it up.

The bride and groom take the opportunity to kiss goodbye before a day of forced separation. With Winter and Logan distracted, I seize the moment and return the teasing favor to Summer.

I pull her behind a corner and press her against the wall. It's a risky move. Anyone could walk by and spot us, but the danger of being caught makes it all the more exciting. I lean in closer, my lips a breath away from hers. I sneak a hand onto her neck, my thumb caressing the skin behind her ear in that way I discovered makes her moan every single time. She has to bite her lip not to now.

Aha, before starting to play the game, she should've remembered I practically invented it.

Never kissing her, I whisper, "I guess I'll see you later," and walk away toward the elevators just as Logan and Winter break their kiss. Tucker still hasn't returned, and Logan and I agree to wait for him.

Summer turns the corner after me and follows her sister into the first available elevator, looking adorably flustered: swollen lips, pink cheeks, and big eyes filled with desire.

I'm congratulating myself for winning this round when she, eyes never leaving mine, slowly tilts her head backward in a seductive gesture while her hands reach up to untie her ponytail. Her long hair cascades down her shoulders in a mesmerizing effect just as her lips part a little. It's a show, all for my benefit. One second before she disappears behind the elevator doors, her parted lips curl up in an evil little grin, leaving me burning in hell.

12

SUMMER

The phantom of Archie's lips is still on mine as I enter my room, and he hasn't even kissed me. The way he pressed me against the wall left my body itching all over, and the worst part is I will have to wait all day to scratch.

To relax the lust a little, I spend forever in the shower and, when I exit, I style my hair in a braid while it's still damp. When we were kids, Winter and I learned this is the most effective hairstyle to go riding with. Leaving your hair loose to catch the wind at a gallop might be scenic, but brushing the knots afterward is a total bitch. Not worth the spectacle.

For the same reason, I wear a pair of stretch jeans, a comfy J. Crew V-neck sweater, and sporty ankle boots—the best alternative to proper riding boots. To go horse riding, it's always best to wear shoes with small heels so they catch on the stirrups and my feet won't slip through.

Lana preemptively texted us hens to come to the bachelorette in sporty casual clothes, and I hope everyone listened. A riding ground might seem like an odd location to host a bachelorette party. But since coming back from Thailand, my sister hasn't stopped complaining about how we never go riding any more since Grandpa passed. So, Lana and I thought this would be the perfect occasion. Not to mention that hairy, four-legged studs will make Winter happier than any stripper ever could.

I finish getting ready well before the designated departure hour, but wait until the very last second to exit my room. Today, I won't be able to avoid bumping into Daria and Susan and Martha, or my bitchy cousins, but at least the sanctimonious aunts won't be at the bachelorette. Still, I'll try to delay the inevitable as much as I can. And I plan to cut the interactions to as short as possible.

Gosh, I need another coffee. I brew myself a cup, smiling as I remember doing the same for Archie a few hours ago. When I'm out of time and excuses to stay hidden in my room, I move down to the lobby.

The bachelorette party bus is already waiting outside and hard to miss. The vehicle is thirty feet long and painted in a rather distinctive bubble-gum pink. Lana outdid herself. I would've never thought of renting something so obnoxiously fun. Heck, I didn't even know they made pink buses.

A familiar pang of regret twists my chest, and for a moment I cannot breathe, remembering how I stabbed Lana in the back, mourning the lost trust and the friendship that will never be the same, even after she's forgiven me. My face heats with shame like it does whenever I think about Johnathan and the affair. I hate what I did; I'd give anything to go back in time and change it. But I can't. The guilt will haunt me until I die. All I can do is own my mistakes, take the lesson home, and do better in the future.

Just as these thoughts writhe furiously inside my head, I lift my gaze and meet Daria's cold stare for the first time since The Mistake. Her mouth curls up in a vicious smile, while she gives me a brief, one-handed wave, saying, "Oh, so you're really here. Haven't seen you around much."

Susan is at her side, foaming at the mouth to see how I'll react.

I could wave back and disappear inside the bus, but what's the point? I can't avoid them forever.

Time to face the music.

I walk straight to them, closing the short distance between us.

"Hi, Daria." I nod at her and then at Susan. "Susy."

Both nod back, half-surprised, half-curious as if I were an animal in a zoo and they were trying to guess my next move.

Daria can't help herself—she was never the stay-quiet type—and speaks first. "Long time no see."

"I know," I say. "And I'm sorry. I wanted to apologize to both of you for disappearing, but after what happened, I was too ashamed to face anyone."

Daria seems surprised at my words, but her gaze doesn't get any less chilly. She also isn't the forgiving type. Even if we don't stand a chance of ever being anything more than casual acquaintances, I still owe her an apology. And I don't know, having Archie not look at me as if I'm disgusting or somehow damaged has made me feel stronger, giving me the backbone to say what I'm about to say. "I did an unforgivable thing; I knew how you felt about cheating and I was too much of a coward to confront you."

"Fair enough," she says. "And what's changed now?"

"Nothing," I say. "I've had time to reflect on my actions and realize that I need to take responsibility for the pain I caused. I don't expect your forgiveness, but I hope you can see that I'm sincere in my apology."

"Yeah, well, apology accepted, Summer." Daria shrugs in a way that tells me, *"You can apologize all you want; we're never going to be friends again."*

"I just want to avoid any drama for my sister's sake. No matter what you think about me, this is her wedding, and I don't want her to worry or feel obligated to come to my rescue."

"No problem," Daria says, with that permanent resting bitch face. *"We know how to behave ourselves."*

The "contrary to you" postscript is clear in her tone.

"Great," I say, looking at Susan. She shrugs in a half-apologetic way, as if to say, *"I might have forgiven you, but Daria would never allow it, so I have to pick sides and I'm not on yours."*

The idea of having lost them saddens me, but being here with them now, I realize I've come to terms with it. Some friendships are stronger than anything while others are simply not meant to last and will crumble under a big enough storm. Daria has had her heart broken by too many cheating men; forgiving me would translate to her as forgiving *them*, and I know she never will.

"That's all I wanted to say," I conclude. "See you around."

I leave them to no doubt gossip behind my back and head onto the bus. We have to leave in five minutes anyway. I go for a seat in the rear as

usual, sitting down with my temples still pulsing from the harrowing
exchange I just had outside.

I hope today will pass fast.

The wish has been barely expressed when my phone pings with an
incoming text from an unknown number.

Eager to find out who it's from, I read the message.

> **FROM ARCHIBALD HILL**
>
> Hope you don't mind, but I finally found a good
> use for the "Winter and Logan Tie the Knot"
> WhatsApp group Tucker created

My stomach does a silly, adolescent flip. Archie searched for my
number, and he's texting me.

Even if I feel as agitated as a teen texting her first crush, I keep my
reply super cool.

> **TO ARCHIE**
>
> Oh, gosh, that group
>
> I mute it every week

With everyone on board, the bus leaves the parking lot just as Archie's
reply comes in.

From Archie:
Every week? I muted it for a year straight off the bat

> **TO ARCHIE**
>
> A year?
>
> LOL
>
> That's badass

> But makes sense, you never replied to a
> single text

> I didn't even know you were in the group

FROM ARCHIE

> Sorry, but the first time Tucker asked us to help research the meaning of flowers and come up with suggestions for the floral arrangements, I had to bail

TO ARCHIE

> But that was a great assignment

> I suggested Gardenias

> They're wedding-white and bringers of joy

FROM ARCHIE

> I remember

> I read the chat from time to time

How weird that I've been texting Archie for months without ever realizing it. Did I write something majorly uncool? I'm tempted to go back and reread the entire thread, but his next text comes in, preventing me.

FROM ARCHIE

> How's it going over there?

The bus is already pulling up at our destination, the riding ground. Wow, that was quick, I barely noticed we were moving.

I read the question again. I could tell Archie about my earlier conversation with Daria and Susan, but I don't want to spoil our chat. Soon I'll be out in the fresh air, riding. And I'm pretty sure only my sister, Lana, and I will make it to the more advanced group—LA isn't famous for its riding grounds, and I bet we're the only ones to have ever been on the back of a horse before. My family, from my mother's side, is originally from Indiana, and my grandparents used to own a ranch near Bloomington. When we were little, Lana, Winter, and I would spend many summers on the farm doing all the Midwestern activities California kids probably never learn: how to ride a horse, how to shoot rifles, crossbows, and every other weapon known to mankind. Or, more harmlessly, how to milk a cow. All important life skills.

Most people, Daria and Susan included, will be stuck in the beginners' practice ring, riding a pony held on a leash by the instructors, while I'll be taking the scenic ride out of the manège.

I finally apologized and got a huge weight off my chest. And if all I am for them now is meat to grind in their gossip machine, there's nothing more I can do about it. I just need to move on and stop dwelling on the past.

So I opt for a flirty reply, teasing Archie with the same double entendre I tortured Logan with last night:

TO ARCHIE
We're about to meet the studs

FROM ARCHIE
Studs?

I was led to believe these would be very PG 13 bachelor and bachelorette parties

TO ARCHIE
What do you mean?

No strippers for you?

FROM ARCHIE

The only thing this bunch would be interested in
seeing stripping is a mummy

And only so that they could properly analyze it
and date the corpse to the right Pharaonic era

TO ARCHIE

Ew

No, seriously, what are you guys doing?

FROM ARCHIE

Gourmet lunch aboard a historic train car while
we reach more wineries to have tastings at

Yawn

You gals?

Once all the hens are gathered in the riding ground courtyard and the
pink-mobile is parked in the visitors lot the manager comes to greet us.
After a short welcoming speech, he asks us to raise hands accordingly to
our riding experience and, as predicted, it's just me, my sister, Lana, and
two female archeologists from Logan's half of the invitation list in the
advanced group.

We follow a boy to the stables where he introduces us to our rides. I'm
with Thunder, a beautiful gray stallion. I pat the horse and caress his
muzzle, whispering small words to get him used to my voice. And while
we familiarize ourselves with each other, I compose a quick reply for
Archie.

TO ARCHIE

I've just met Thunder

He's going to be my ride today

Archie replies with a yellow emoji holding its chin questioningly.

FROM ARCHIE

That's a very bad name, even for a male stripper

I chuckle; time to put the guy out of his misery. I lean my face next to my equine companion and snap a selfie. I caption the pic: Archie, meet Thunder.

Archie's reply is a head-exploding emoji.

In the background, the tour guide calls for everyone who's going on the long ride to gather at the trail entrance. I grab Thunder by the reins and guide him out of the stables, following behind my sister's and Lana's rides.

Before mounting, I compose a quick text for Archie.

TO ARCHIE

We're about to leave

The guide has asked us not to use our phones while on the trail

They have a history of people getting distracted and falling off their horses

Talk later?

I'll be gone for about two hours

A reply comes within seconds.

FROM ARCHIE

Those are going to be two long hours

His words make my heart flutter. Even more when they're followed by a cat-face emoji blowing me a kiss. This guy is unbelievable. So big and strong, with the bad-boy bike and everything, sending me kiss-blowing catmojis. I shake my head. He's sure full of surprises.

At times, I feel like he's just being flirty and having a good time. At others, I feel like we're crossing boundaries we said we wouldn't cross. I mean, is this normal behavior for a relationships-avoiding, incorrigible bachelor?

Or is he like this just with me?

That's a dangerous thought to have, that Archie is different with me, and I should be careful not to rely too much on it because he'd never commit. After all, he made sure the boundaries were clear from the start —no strings attached between us. But those boundaries become more difficult to keep in check when he sends me messages like that. Or keeps being so sweet. Or spoons me in bed. It's confusing, and yet, it feels so good.

I push the thoughts to the back of my mind as I store my phone in the saddle's pocket made for this specific purpose, and then place my right foot into the corresponding stirrup to haul myself atop Thunder.

The ride is as scenic and filled with breathtaking vistas as advertised. Still, nagging questions about Archie's intentions keep flying through my mind like the ever-changing landscape of the tour. But I do my best to ignore them. I've lived obsessed with the past for the last year, I won't trade that fixation for one about the future. I should try to live more in the present.

As we make our way through the trail, Thunder's powerful gallop takes me back to the ranch in Indiana. Memories of my grandparents, my cousins, and the horses we rode flood my mind. The cold wind hits my face, and I close my eyes, inhaling deeply the scent of nature around me.

We continue riding until we reach an open field. The guide instructs us to halt our horses and dismount.

"We're stopping for a short break," he says. "Feel free to explore while we rest."

I stretch my legs as I dismount from Thunder. Lana walks toward a nearby tree, and she leans against it, taking out her phone to check her messages. Archie won't have written to me since I told him I'd be gone for two hours. So I leave Lana to it and go look for my sister.

I find Winter sitting on a rock, gazing out at the horizon with a serene expression on her face. I walk up to her and sit down beside her, taking in the view myself. We sit in comfortable silence, watching the sun glow over the beautiful valley.

"You know, I'm really proud of you," Winter says suddenly, breaking the silence.

I turn to look at her, surprised. "Why?"

"You've been handling everything so well lately. I know it's been tough, but you're really starting to move forward and let go of the past," she says, giving my shoulder a reassuring squeeze.

I smile at her, feeling grateful for her support. "Thanks, sis. That means a lot."

We sit there a while longer until Lana calls out to us that it's time to head back. As we mount our horses and follow the guide toward the stables, I can't help but feel a sense of peace wash over me. Maybe Winter is right; maybe I am starting to let go of the past and move forward. And maybe that's thanks in part to Archie and the unexpected connection we share.

My heart skips a beat just thinking about him. It's moments like this that make me wonder if there could be something more between us than just a casual fling. But I push those thoughts aside and focus on enjoying the present moment with my sister and friends.

Once we arrive back at the ranch, we are spoiled with a perfect pairing of estate wines served with an assortment of cheeses, charcuterie, spreads, fruit, and nuts.

Honestly, Napa is ruining wine for me. How will I ever go back to drinking regular, run-of-the-mill wines? My palate is getting used to America's best.

Unbidden, my treacherous brain follows that same train of thought, but in a different, dangerous direction. *How will I ever go back to dating regular, run-of-the-mill guys?* Archie is the Cabernet Sauvignon of dating. He'll ruin men for me.

In search of a distraction from these ever-disturbing thoughts, I finally pay attention to the estate's sommelier as he explains the tasting notes of the vintage we're sipping.

"You'll find rich flavors of blackberries and black plum, dried herbs, sweet oak spices, vanilla beans, and toasted almonds. Take another sip," the sommelier instructs. "Appreciate how all these aromas unfold in mesmerizing layers, sending a wave of deliciously intense complexity across the palate in a tasty expression of power and elegance."

But hearing the wine's merits is no use as a diversion. My mind keeps associating everything with Archie. In the few short days I've known him,

I've realized Archie has just as many layers of complexity as the wine in my glass. He can be both sweet and strong. But also the most attentive, considerate, well-mannered man, only to transform into a sexual animal two hours later. Still alert to my every need, but definitely not poised about satisfying them.

And I can't ignore the newfound confidence in myself he's given me. Not like dating Johnathan did, like I felt grateful someone would consider me worthy of their love. Archie has promised me no love, no feelings, and yet, he's made me feel better about myself. Stronger, freer. Like I have a right to be happy again.

And let's not forget those washboard abs. I know it's a superficial feature compared to his other qualities, but, gosh, I've never seen abs so defined in real life. The muscles are so hard I could grate any of these cheeses on them. And ours is just a fling so it's okay for me to be a little superficial and relish the most perfect six-pack I'll ever touch.

"Most of these characteristics," the sommelier continues, "can be attributed to the magical nature surrounding us. Here, our grapes thrive on ideal soil and perfectly balanced weather conditions with just the right amount of sunlight and rain."

Mmm. That makes me reflect on how I don't know much about Archie's background. My knowledge stops at the groom-related basics: he and Logan met in college and have stuck together ever since, merging their friendship with their professional lives. But what of his life before college, of his family, or of where he went to high school? Who was his first kiss? What was his major in college? How did he become an adventurer? I want to discover all of this and more about him. Will I have the time? A few days seem too short a period to satisfy my curiosity.

Hey, you'll see him again. He's your sister's soon-to-be-husband's best friend. Your paths will cross sooner or later

Yeah, especially since I hope to be moving to the Bay Area soon to be closer to my sister. But the intimacy of this week? That will be gone. He won't be whispering sweet nothings in my ears and cuddling me to sleep. Or making me bite on the pillow to stop myself from screaming his name and waking up the entire hotel. All of that will be gone. He'll probably be doing it with someone else.

The thought causes a dark swirl of nausea in my stomach. Oh, gosh, there I go again; I have to stop obsessing. I concentrate back on the wine explanation. I look around and everybody else seems keen on listening. Am I the only distracted one? Well, I'm probably the only one having a secret affair with the best man.

"But good soil is not all it takes to make superb wine," the sommelier carries on. "There's a science to turning perfect grapes into a perfect wine. First, we hand-harvest them with three stages of strict sorting: on the vine, then by individual clusters, and then again by single berry following the de-stemming. The grapes that make the cut are then moved into traditional French oak tanks for cold soak, fermentation, and extended maceration..."

Try to concentrate as I might, I'm helpless. As the explanation continues, I zone out again, my thoughts inexorably returning to Archie. I cringe as I contemplate the number of women it took to make Archie such a great lover. If a Cabernet Sauvignon takes twenty months of barrel aging to reach its final, perfect blend, I wonder how many years Archie had to play the field to become as skilled as he is today?

And why do I have to obsess about his past? Can't I just enjoy the final product?

Yes, I can, and I should. But again, just as with the wine, I'm getting used to the best and it will be hard to go back to dating ordinary men. That is, once I'm ready to dip my toes in the dating pool again.

Mmm...

I bet no one can grow a beard as soft as his.

Oh, do we like beards now? a little prickly voice asks in my head.

Not beards, plural, only a very specific one.

Hon, you sound like someone who's bitten off more than she can chew, the voice replies.

I sigh, silently agreeing with my conscience.

13

SUMMER

Tonight the bachelor and bachelorette parties are supposed to merge. *Yay!* The resort has cordoned off a wide area near the pool and reserved it for the wedding party. The weather is playing along, making it okay, with the help of a few strategically placed patio heaters, to eat outdoors. Dinner is going to be self-serve, and the menu is all things barbecue: steaks, hamburgers, hot dogs, ribs, grilled chicken, and vegetable shish kebabs. There's even a seafood station with grilled shrimp and salmon. The various grilling stations are assembled in a semicircle at the end of the patio, and each has its dedicated cook while baskets of French fries are being brought outside from the indoor kitchen.

A server with a round, heavy-looking tray offers me a basket, and I gladly take it.

Biting down on a fry, I search the crowd for Archie. Same as I used to do back in high school when I had a secret crush on David Montgomery and spent every minute searching the halls, cafeteria, and any other common space for him. Just seeing David would mark whether my day had been a great one or a complete waste of time. If we crossed ways in the halls, I'd get butterflies. If I sat at a table next to his in the cafeteria and was able to overhear some of his conversations with his friends, I'd become so ecstatic I wouldn't touch any food.

Sadly, David and I never kissed. Heck, he never even talked ,to me. David was a senior, and I was a freshman; he graduated the next year and disappeared from my life forever. But tonight, not only will I get to talk to my crush, and to kiss him as many times as I want, we'll touch all the bases. I only have to be patient. My toes curl in anticipation. Archie and I haven't been naked together since yesterday afternoon; more than a day, and definitely too long.

I keep scanning the crowd, but no sign of the best man. Instead, I spot my sister and Logan seated at one of the round tables, plates loaded with food already in front of them. Shortly afterward, Lana and Tucker also join them. My best bet is to sit with them and hope Archie will do the same, just like at breakfast, recreating the unofficial wedding party table. A perfect way for Archie and me to have dinner together without being conspicuous.

As I navigate the mass of guests cramming the patio, I'm a lot calmer than I would have been a few days ago. I've apologized to Daria, and even if my words fell on deaf ears, I tried. I also don't care as much as I used to about what people think of me. The Mistake, if nothing else, has forced me to take a hard look at my life. I thought I had a solid circle of friends, but when it all came tumbling down, only two people were left by my side: Winter and, ironically enough, Lana—the person who should've thrown me to the wolves and was the first to forgive me instead.

I grab a cold beer from an ice bucket and join my sister's table.

"Hey," I say. "The grill smells amazing. What are you guys having?"

Chewing down a bite of hamburger, my sister says, "I'm having every-thing. The ribs are divine, and this hamburger is unbelievable." Winter licks a bit of BBQ sauce off her fingers and promptly takes another enor-mous chomp.

I smile to myself. I love that my sister is not one of those brides obsessed about being a size zero, and that she hasn't lost her appetite because of the upcoming nuptials. Plus, the cheeses and cold cuts we had for lunch at the ranch, while tasteful and curated, lacked in quantity—especially after a day spent outdoors.

Famished, I move to the back of the line for the grills and grab an empty plate from the stash near the first station, my stomach grumbling in anticipation. I load my plate with a bit of everything and turn, ready to go back to the table.

That's when I see him.

Archie is standing on the threshold, between the big French doors leading outside from within the hotel. The patio is three steps down from those doors, granting me an unobstructed view of Archie in his raised position. He's looking chill in a plaid short-sleeved button-down shirt and white cargo shorts.

Honestly, he's just missing a shark-teeth necklace to be the perfect Surfer Boy, another great fantasy of mine. I add the image to my mental catalog of his outfits, undecided on what guise is my favorite. Probably still the one that doesn't require any clothes.

His eyes search the crowd, moving over the heads of the people assembled below until they finally come to rest on me. When he spots me, his entire face brightens up in an open smile, and my empty stomach has its usual reaction and promptly explodes with butterflies, making those I used to experience for David Montgomery feel like amateur hour.

Archie cuts through the throng of people, heading straight for me, and only stops a step short when the giant plate loaded with meat standing between us forces him to. It's good I'm holding this thing in my hands or I would've thrown my arms around his neck already and blown our cover.

"Hey," I say.

"Hey, yourself."

I inch the plate toward Logan and Winter's table. "I'm sitting with my sister over there."

"I'll grab some food and come join you."

I nod, and am about to brush past him when he leans down and whispers in my ear, "Nice dress, by the way."

A cold shiver spider walks down my spine while my face heats up. I'll admit I made a bit more of an effort than I usually would for a casual barbecue evening. I'm wearing a white sundress with a pineapple print, not exactly vintage, but with a retro, elegant feel. The dress has a V neckline and is sleeveless; it ties behind the neck in a bow it took me twenty minutes to shape in perfect symmetry. The skirt is wide and knee-length, while the waist is tight for that great fit-flare silhouette effect that flatters my figure. My hair is arranged atop my head in a deceivingly messy giant bun I spent half an hour sculpturing—I call it the Hepburn. To complete the outfit, I've put on killer-heel strappy sandals. I went easy on the makeup only because I don't want to leave it all smeared on Archie's pillow later tonight. Instead, I pampered my skin with a gentle scrub and a facial mask, and I'm only wearing a layer of transparent mascara and ChapStick.

But the hungry way Archie keeps looking at me throughout dinner makes me feel as beautiful as if a professional had done my makeup. Being in public with him when we can't kiss or touch or do anything other than play with subtle stares is an unbearable form of torture. And dinner tonight is no different.

We spend the whole evening eye-flirting with each other in what is an hours-long, hands-off foreplay session. I don't pay much attention to what everyone else is saying; it's mostly anecdotes from the day. Half of them I already know from personal experience, and the other half is not as interesting or amusing enough to tear my concentration away from Archie's lips. From his sizzling, icy stare. From those big hands...

I'm desperately trying to find a polite way to leave as soon as all the plates are empty when Tucker gives everyone the perfect excuse.

"Guys," he says, standing up and stretching his arms. "I'm super tired. I'm calling it an early night."

"Are you sure?" Logan asks. "We can sleep in tomorrow; nothing but a spa day ahead."

"No, I know, but I'm positively beaten." He chuckles awkwardly. "Must be all the wine."

Archie throws his friend a stare that, if I had to define, I'd call suspicious. But he's also just as quick to jump on the "going to bed early" wagon.

As he gets up, his devilish grin promises a whole lot of fun activities to take place in said bed, none of which include sleep.

"If you're going, I'm going, too," Archie says.

Winter narrows her eyes at him. "To bed? Alone? This early?"

"That'd be correct."

"Why aren't you trying to sleep with any of the female guests? Are you ill?"

I cringe at the stark reminder I'm only one of many previous conquests. Yet, I shake the thought away. This week he's all mine, and I will enjoy the ride while it lasts.

Archie winces at being put on the spot. "Subtle much?"

"No, honestly," Winter insists. "What's up with you?"

"Maybe I already have a rendezvous arranged and was trying to leave politely without drawing attention," he says, making my face catch fire. I hide it behind a glass of water, compose my features into the mother of all poker faces, and dare a peek at my sister. She's completely oblivious and hasn't looked my way once.

"Really?" Winter asks. "And who's the lucky lady?"

"A true gentleman doesn't kiss and tell," Archie replies.

I almost roll my eyes, but catch myself at the last second, my gaze landing on Lana. And, oh my gosh, she's staring at me slightly wide-eyed, kind of slack jawed, as if she's just connected all the wrong dots. I try to telepathically send her a "please keep quiet" plea, and she must receive the message because her lips press together into a furtive half-smile and she gives me the tiniest of nods.

After some more badgering from my sister to find out who Archie's conquest is, and more stubborn refusals from Archie to fess up, he and Tucker finally walk away, leaving me in need of a fresh excuse to beat it.

But now I can't go. Not after Archie has openly admitted he's seeing someone. I want to avoid arousing any suspicion in my sister's head. I have to. At. All. Costs. Sorry, Surfer Archie will have to wait a while before I can safely join him in his room.

I'm already resigned to this sad destiny when Lana, unexpectedly, comes to the rescue. Giving me that secretive half-smile again, she stands up, saying, "Guys, I'm going to call it a night as well."

"Not you, too," Winter protests. "What's your excuse?"

"Christian has been busy shooting all day and I haven't spoken to him yet. Now is the only good time to talk."

I can't honestly say how much truth laces Lana's statement. Does she really plan to call Christian, or is she leaving so that I, too, can leave without giving my sister the wrong impression?

Before I can decide on an answer, the maid of honor blows us kisses and is on her way off to the hotel.

Now or never.

I stand up. "Well, you guys, as much as I'd love to stay and be the third wheel all night, I'm going to go, too."

Winter snorts. "Don't be ridiculous. You'll never be a third wheel with me."

"I was joking," I say. The last thing I want is to make my sister uncomfortable. "But you guys haven't seen each other all day. I'd understand if you wanted to go *rest* a little."

Not taking the hint, Winter replies, "I'm not that tired."

Thankfully, the groom-to-be seems to be more on board with my let's-ditch-the-barbecue-and-go-have-sex agenda, even if he doesn't know I'm sharing the same urges.

Logan yawns quite theatrically and gives my sister *the* look, saying, "Actually, I could use some nappy time."

The bride finally gets the message, and suddenly an early bedtime becomes appealing to her, too.

She looks up at me. "Are you sure you don't want to hang out a little longer?"

"Positive. You kids go have fun," I say, using the tone a benevolent aunt would use when sending her horny niece to fool around—as if I didn't have a vested, adult-turned-randy-teen interest in the game.

I kiss Winter goodnight, wink at Logan, then rush inside and toward the elevators before anyone can stop me.

When Archie opens his door five minutes later, he greets me with an infuriating, "What took you so long?"

I jokingly poke him in the chest with a finger while pushing him into the room. "Well, next time try not to mention a secret romantic rendezvous in front of my sister and I'll be faster."

"She was hounding me like a dog; I had to throw her a bone."

"Because it'd be so impossible for you not to get laid." I try to make my comment sound playful and teasing, but the words come out more nagging than I intended.

"I have a healthy sex life; what's wrong with that?"

"I don't know, you tell me." I hate the tone of my voice as I speak, how it sounds all but indifferent.

Archie shrugs in a non-answer.

So, I prod him a little more. "If I remember correctly, you came back from the trip to Thailand empty-handed. No conquests made."

He comes dangerously close to me. "That's because I had met the wrong Knowles twin."

"Oh, so now I'm the *right* Knowles twin?"

"Why are you being like this?" Archie frowns. "Did I do something wrong?"

"No, no. It's not you. I just realized I don't know anything about you." I throw my hands up, a little exasperated. "Where are you from? What was your major in college? Who was your first kiss?"

"I don't know those things about you either."

Right. Because this isn't that kind of relationship.

Archie walks closer to me, his fingertips brushing up my arms. "Can't you be okay just knowing how much I want you right now?"

He drops a kiss on my neck and all coherent thought is lost to me. Why were we arguing?

"Knowing how much this little bow at the back of your neck has been teasing me all night," Archie whispers. "I've so been looking forward to untying it." He pulls at the strings unbearably slowly, eyes locked on mine.

I shift my gaze lower, to his lips, and he puts me out of my misery with a deep kiss just as my dress slips down my body and pools at my feet.

His hands travel up my sides, tracing invisible patterns on my skin. As his thumbs stroke the bare skin of my back, goosebumps rise all over my body. I shiver even when the heat between us is palpable, and I find myself struggling to catch my breath. With a soft moan, I part my lips for him, and he deepens the kiss. He tastes of desire, and the promise of a night I'm never going to forget.

Breaking the kiss, I push back from him and step out of the dress pool.

I'm left standing only in my high heels and underwear, exposed but not embarrassed. To be honest, I've never felt sexier.

"Certain things are worth waiting for," I say.

Archie's eyes darken with desire, and he scoops me up into his arms. "I've been waiting for you for a long time."

14

ARCHIE

A few earth-shattering orgasms later, I'm on my belly about ready to pass out when Summer trails her fingertips over my naked butt cheeks. The soft caresses have me alert again at once.

"Are these the scars from your injury in Thailand?" she asks.

"Yep," I say, not moving. Feeling glad for the first time that my ass got filleted last year.

"How did you get them again?"

"If I told you I fought a panther to the death, would you believe me?"

"And she went just for the ass? Smart kitty." Summer chuckles. "But I remember Winter telling me it was something way more ridiculous. Didn't you just fall flat on a thorny bush or something?"

"It was palmetto palms and they weren't thorns, they were spears, I needed twenty-five stitches overall."

"Oh, poor baby." Summer proceeds to kiss every single one of the scars. When one kiss turns into a soft bite, sleep becomes the farthest thing from my mind.

In a split second, I roll over and pin her underneath me. "What are you doing?"

"Sorry. I've always been an ass girl. What does it for you?"

Sexy blondes with a dirty mouth apparently.

"You, baby," I say without thinking. "You are all I ever wanted."

And before any of us can process what I just said, I silence her with a kiss.

Sleep never felt more overrated.

* * *

A sense of unease wakes me up. I stir in bed, my hand automatically reaching for Summer. She's still lying next to me, so I wrap my arms around her, sighing in relief. The ease is short-lived, though, as I realize it was the fear she'd be gone again that woke me. The concept settles a little heavy on my chest, along with a memory from last night: me scooping Summer into my arms, saying, "I've been waiting for you for a long time." Or "You are all I ever wanted."

What did I mean by that? And did my words give the wrong impression? Does Summer have expectations now? Do I? To be honest, I'm not looking forward to that Sunday end-mark at all. Three more nights to spend with her seems too short a time.

Summer stirs, eyes still closed. Gosh, she's beautiful. Not that she hasn't always been beautiful, but I don't know... It's as if she's becoming more so every day. Hard to explain, but the more I stare at her, the more perfect she looks. Because she is perfect, and not just in a physical sense. Summer is fun, and a little quirky sometimes. But she's also smart and kind and sweet. And all other women compared to her fade into the background.

Heck, Scarlett Johansson could walk past that door right now and I wouldn't spare her a second glance.

And that, my friend, is an even scarier thought. One I shouldn't contemplate without being properly caffeinated.

I return yesterday's favor and make coffee. Summer's I leave black, bringing the tiny creamer pod and a sugar packet along with her cup to leave her the choice of what to add, just like she did for me yesterday.

As I sit on the bed again, either the movement or the coffee scent wakes her. Summer stretches, hands closed in fists near her head, elbows spread wide on the pillow.

"Morning," she says, pushing up into a sitting position. "Is that coffee I smell?"

"Yep." I give her the cup and accessories. "I don't know how you like it."

She smiles, adding both the creamer and sugar. "Sweet and full of milk, thank you."

"Only returning the favor."

Summer takes a long sip, saying nothing. Guess we're not discussing why she sneaked out of my bedroom while I was still sleeping yesterday and made me wake up to an empty bed and a cup of coffee. What else are we avoiding telling each other? A lot, I fear. Too much.

"Yoga will start soon. You want to go?" I ask, steering clear of more serious topics like a coward.

"Yeah, sure," she says. "I'll pop into my room real quick to get changed and meet you downstairs."

"Okay." I get up and pretend to use the bathroom to give her some privacy. When I walk out she's in the white dress again, feet bare, the heels dangling from her fingers. The temptation to untie that bow behind her neck again and skip yoga altogether is hard to resist, but I bite the inside of my cheek and act cool. "See you in a bit?"

"Sure," she says, blushing. My eyes must be saying what my mouth isn't.

Summer walks toward me, stands on tiptoe, and stamps a sweet kiss on my lips. It's an almost innocent gesture, but it has a lot of meaning for me that she didn't just walk out of the room.

In yoga, our work has improved yet again. Our motions are perfectly coordinated, we're more familiar with the various poses, and we move through them flawlessly. Our bodies seem to recognize each other, and as Summer stares into my eyes openly as I lift her up, the sense of belonging extends beyond the physical. The idea that I've let things go too far terrifies me a little.

But I don't know how else to be with her.

"Wonderful job, you guys," the instructor says, walking past us toward the end of class. "You make a great team."

The simple comment launches me into another mental rant. Are we a team? I feel a little that way, like it's me and Summer against the world.

And not just because we're keeping our involvement a secret. But I can't help but wonder what that means for us. She's going back to LA on Sunday and I'm going back to Berkley. That's what I want, right?

But as we walk to the breakfast room, this insane thought pops into my head that I'd rather not have to share her with the rest of the wedding party. Not for breakfast. And not for anything else.

Last night, Logan said he wanted to sleep in, so there might be a chance he and Winter are still in bed.

That hope dies when I spot my friend's mop of black hair next to Tucker's distinctive brown curls.

So much for taking it easy, I think accusingly.

My dream of breakfast for two at a table by the window, eating croissants and enjoying the view together, vanishes. Summer will want to keep up appearances.

Sucks. Especially because today's activities will be split by gender again. Unfortunately, the resort keeps separate spas for men and women. That's probably better, though. I don't think I'd be able to survive watching Summer strut around in a bikini and keep my hands to myself. But maybe we could bail early from the spa day and go somewhere else, just the two of us.

Here's another funny thought: I want to spend the day with Summer. Clothes on or off, I don't care. And since when have I ever wanted to be with a woman beyond the bedroom?

Never. Ever.

Not for long, at least. And never as fiercely.

I mope over all these new realizations through our crowded breakfast, until Summer gets up to refill her plate and I subtly follow.

I wait until we're near the pastry counter to lean into her body, appreciating the jolt of surprise that shakes her, and the consequent relaxation when she realizes it's me. The food tables are all placed behind a corner and no one else is around, granting me a little more flirting space.

"Off to the spa soon?" I say.

"Mm-hm," she hums.

"I feel sorry for those massage therapists."

"Why?" She frowns, popping a bite-sized donut into her mouth.

I wiggle my fingers. "They'll have to compete with these babies."

"Ah, I can give you a rematch anytime you want."

Summer piles more sweets onto her plate and turns to walk back to our table. I make to follow, but, as if sensing I'm trailing her like a puppy, she stops and looks at me over her shoulder. "You'd better fill a plate with something."

She blows me a kiss and doesn't wait for me.

I grab an empty plate and pile it with pastries from the closest tray, before returning to our table. But the moment I sit down, Logan looks up at me with a frown.

"Since when do you eat raisins?"

I stare down at my plate and recoil in horror at finding it filled with mini cinnamon swirls riddled with raisins.

"I—I don't mind them that much lately." And to prove my point, I grab one of the mini buns and bite half off. The pastry and cinnamon aren't that bad, but there's no escaping the chewy, disgusting, too-sweet taste of the raisins. There are a ton of them, too, ruining a perfectly good breakfast treat and making me want to puke in my mouth. But I can't, so I try to keep a straight face and, like a martyr, swallow.

Logan shrugs and goes back to eating his eggs, ignorant of the trial he just put me through, while Summer has to hide a smile behind her mug of coffee.

I make the other half of the pastry discreetly disappear into my napkin, and wash away the awful aftertaste with coffee.

* * *

A few hours later, I'm wandering around the spa's indoor pool with contraband hidden in my robe's pocket.

Spa guests are not supposed to bring phones into the relaxation area, but I'm half bored to death and my only hope for a distraction is to text Summer.

TO SUMMER

This day is the worst

Little chance of getting her to reply, as I'm sure phones are also banned on the female side of the spa, but what can I say? I'm an optimist by nature.

Half an hour later, while I lie in a chaise sipping my third herbal tea of the day, a soft vibration shakes my pocket. I check the screen and see with a jolt of pleasure that it's a text from Summer.

FROM SUMMER
Why? Did your massage suck or something?

Leaning on my side to shelter the phone from view with my back, I compose a quick reply.

TO SUMMER
No, I was talking about food. I had to eat those stupid raisins at breakfast and now all they're giving me to drink is herbal tea

FROM SUMMER
Herbal tea is actually good for you. But I get why you're not a fan of raisins

TO SUMMER
They're the worst invention ever made

Why would someone in their right mind take nice grapes and turn them into shriveled-down dead droppings set free into the world to ruin all the best foods?

Summer sends me an emoji of a crying and laughing cat.

FROM SUMMER
I hate them only when I grab a cookie thinking it's chocolate chips and find raisins instead

· · ·

TO SUMMER

Oh, that's the worst

How's the spa day going?

FROM SUMMER

I snuck into the locker room

I already had my massage and if I stayed in a
Jacuzzi any longer I'd be sprouting gills

TO SUMMER

Can you get away unnoticed?

FROM SUMMER

Why? Can you?

TO SUMMER

Say the word and I'm outta here

I delete the answer and re-type it three times. I stare at it, letting my thumb hang over the send button. Am I making a mistake here?

"Sir?" A spa attendant approaches me with a tray. "Would you like more tea?"

I turn to look over my shoulder, doing my best to keep my phone hidden under my chaise, and shake my head. "No, thanks."

If I drink any more tea I'll turn into a tea bag myself.

Without thinking, I hit send and wait for Summer's reply.

FROM SUMMER

> Let me check where my sister's at real quick

The screen remains black for a few unbearably long minutes before another series of texts arrive in rapid succession.

FROM SUMMER

> Winter is getting her massage now

> Then she has a facial, waxing, and a full mani-pedi booked

> She'll be busy for hours

> My room or yours?

15

SUMMER

The massage and spa day were relaxing, but not as relaxing as Archie taking care of me *multiple times* afterward.

I stretch in bed, unwilling to get up, but I must.

"I have to go," I say.

"Mmm?" Archie raises his head from its resting spot on my chest. "Why?"

"Another lovely dinner with my parents."

Technically, this should've been a meal for both the bride's and groom's families, but since Logan sadly lost his parents young, my dad will be the sole host.

"Oh, yeah," he says, dropping his chin just below my collarbone, "it's on the schedule."

I look down at him. "You mean *your* schedule, too?"

Archie's hands move to my sides, threatening to tickle me. "Don't tell me you've muted the WhatsApp group again?"

To be honest, lately, I haven't paid much attention to anything on my phone except for Archie's texts. "I might've. Why?"

"The entire wedding party is invited."

"Oh, you're going to meet my parents." I say the words before thinking of their meaning and immediately retract them. "I didn't mean anything by that."

"Relax," he says. "No one knows about us; all the heat will be on the groom."

He's right, and I have no reason to be nervous. But I still am... At least, until Archie's hands start to play a very different game from tickle monster, moving down from my sides to my hips while he kisses my neck.

"Do you think we have time for another—"

"No," I say, before he can convince me to be late. "I have to go back to my room, shower, and get ready."

He bites my earlobe. "We could shower together."

It takes all my force of will to resist the temptation and get out of bed, but I have to. I already left the spa early. If I'm late to dinner, I worry Winter will suspect I'm up to something.

I end up being so on time that only my parents are seated at the table when I arrive at the restaurant. We're at the fancy one tonight. A separate building from the main hotel, with an English countryside décor: all dark woods and fabric-shaded table lamps.

Tucker arrives next. Then Lana, the happy couple, and last but not late, Archie. At first, I don't recognize him as he walks toward our table. He's dressed ridiculously primly, clad in a pair of white jeans and a light-blue V-neck sweater. Tonight's fantasy would be: member of a nineties boy band. If nineties boy bands ever allowed for beards. Mmm, I'm not sure about this one. The good-boy look is weird on him. But—and this is a big but—it's the perfect outfit a boyfriend would wear to meet his girlfriend's parents for the first time.

And I have to stop thinking like that. Yes, the guy I've been sleeping with for the past few days will have dinner with my parents tonight, but he definitely isn't here in a boyfriend capacity.

"Hello, *Dawson's Creek*," my sister greets him, probably sharing my idea that his clothes look out of character. "Where did you leave your *E.T.* poster? In your bedroom next to *Jurassic Park* and *Jaws*?"

"Oh, come on, Snowflake, you must know my favorite Spielberg movies are the *Indiana Jones*," he quips right back, and am I irked he has a nickname for my sister but not for me? Would I like him to call me buttercup, cupcake, sunflower? Honestly, no, yikes. "You're the most glowing bride as always," Archie concludes.

His smile is wide and charming, and his manners impeccable, especially as he rounds the table to shake my father's hand and kiss my mom's after officially introducing himself. If I didn't know better, I'd say he was trying to impress my parents. Mom, for one, has melted at the hand-kissing.

He finally sits down at the only free spot left between Lana and Winter, across the table from me. I'm in between Tucker, who has Logan on his other side, and my dad, who's also sitting next to my mom.

Once it's clear we're not expecting anyone else, the server, who has been looming close by since I arrived, brings our menus and asks if we're ready to order drinks. I sure am, and ask for an apple martini. If I have to endure an entire dinner with Archie and my parents seated at the same table, I need something stronger than wine or beer.

Everybody at the table is pretty chatty, allowing me to take a back seat in the conversation and cull my nerves in private, while doling out the odd comment here and there.

After delivering our drinks, the server comes back shortly afterward to take everyone's orders. I go with the Asian-style tuna steak, while I note Archie orders a bone-in fillet.

Dad is charged with choosing the wine for the table, not because he has any specific competence on the subject, but by simple merits of seniority.

The server has just left with the table's orders when Logan's phone starts ringing. He takes it out of his pocket and checks the screen, his eyes going wide. But he's quick to hide the surprise as he silences the phone and puts it face down on the table.

But not two minutes later, the phone starts vibrating again.

"Darling," my mom says. "Don't worry, if it's something important you can take the call."

"Nah, it's an international call." Logan squirms in his chair. "Could be work; I'll call back later."

"International? Couldn't it be one of your guests needing something?" my mom asks. "Have they all arrived?"

Still uneasy, Logan says, "No, but I'm sure it's not one of my guests."

"How can you know?"

"Country code. We don't have anyone coming in from North Africa."

Winter, voice cold as ice, asks, "Which country in *North Africa* are they calling from?"

Her fiancé holds the phone in one hand while scratching the back of his head with the other as he replies, "Egypt."

A wave of discomfort ripples through the table.

Ah.

After she came back from Thailand, Winter told me everything about Logan's ex, Tara Something. She's a hard-ass archeologist who made a monumental discovery in the Valley of Kings in Egypt and who's still living in Africa. We spent an entire afternoon Google-stalking her, and I suspect my sister even bought her book, a non-fiction account of her discovery, and read it.

The phone goes silent only to start vibrating again a second later.

My dad inches his chin toward it. "Seems like they really need to talk to you?" Then he turns to the table. "Isn't it like what, the middle of the night in Egypt?"

"Must be dawn," Logan says. "Excavation work starts early." He peers at the insistently vibrating phone and adds, "Maybe I should get this in private. I wouldn't want to disturb you all."

"Oh, it's no trouble at all," my mom says, oblivious to the underlying tension between the bride and groom-to-be.

Winter hasn't spoken since the word "Egypt" crossed Logan's lips, and she's now giving him the stare of death, daring him to get up and go talk to his ex *in private.*

Desperate, Logan stares at his best friend for help. Archie gives him a subtle shake of the head that I interpret as a, "No, dude, you'd better keep your ass glued to that chair if you want to speak with your ex who you haven't heard from in years."

Logan must understand the same unspoken message because, with a resigned sigh, he picks up. "Hello."

"Hey."

Tara's is a simple greeting, but the tone is loaded with familiarity and a shared past. Unfortunately for the groom, the voice on the other side is loud enough for everyone at the table to hear and pick up on these details. Also, we're all keeping a religious silence as we shamelessly eavesdrop on the conversation. And even if we weren't, I suspect Winter would kill anyone who dared utter a sound in cold blood.

"Err, how have you been?" Logan asks.

"Oh, you know," Tara says. "Busy. Lots of cataloging going on, and the work on the new museum is crazy. I've switched the exposition around a thousand times to find the perfect order of presentation and still can't decide, even if I know patrons won't care or notice that much," she rants on, clearly nervous. "You must have the same troubles in Thailand."

Logan lets out an awkward chuckle. "Oh, no. We got lucky; the government threw a boatload of money at us and we're just working on opening the final wing of the exposition."

"I can't wait to see it," Tara says. I look at my sister's face, and it's like Winter has turned to stone. "From what I've heard, it's magnificent."

"I hope so," Logan says, the portrait of a man who'd gladly crawl out of his skin.

Silence stretches on the line until Tara speaks again. "I heard congratulations are in order. You're getting married?"

The question seems to be loaded, in a "have you truly forgotten about me?" way.

"Yes," Logan says, staring directly at my sister, "to the most wonderful woman on Earth, the day after tomorrow."

Another protracted pause, and then Tara speaks in a small voice, "Well, as I said, congratulations. I have to go now; they need me at the museum. Goodbye, Logan."

The ex hangs up before he has time to reply, prompting the entire table to let go of a collective breath of relief.

Logan turns to Winter. "I'm sorry," he says. "She hasn't called me in years. I thought something bad might've happened."

My sister swallows and nods. "It's okay," she says. "I just feel sorry for her."

"Why?" Logan asks, looking puzzled.

"Because Tara has realized she was the dumbest cow to dump you for a stupid pharaoh's tomb, and now she's too late."

They kiss. And it's not a chaste peck on the lips. It's a real, deep, long kiss that prompts my dad to cough and hide his face in his napkin.

They're so in love, it's disgusting. I can't help but steal a glance at Archie, and find him observing me. When our eyes meet, he winks, causing my stomach to do a silly little flip.

And I have such a crush, *I'm* disgusting.

When the betrothed couple finally break their kiss, my sister's good mood seems completely restored.

Winter places her napkin on her legs, asking, "What are you guys all doing tomorrow?"

"Tomorrow?" I ask, on edge. "Friday is a free day, right?" This afternoon, Archie and I made plans to have lunch in Yountville, and maybe visit a vineyard or brewery together. And I don't want Winter's well-meaning desire for conviviality to ruin the plan. "We don't have any mandatory activities."

I flash a panicked stare at Archie, and if eyes could talk, his would be saying, *"Sheesh, woman, be cool."*

On his left, Winter pouts. "I'm sorry a *mandatory* spa day has been so hard on you. Where did you disappear to, anyway?"

"I had a work call," I lie.

"I thought phones weren't allowed."

"No, but I went to the locker room to check my messages and had to call the office back."

"So, what are you doing with your *free* day, then? More work?" She's being passive-aggressive.

"No, I just planned on seeing the sights. Nothing in particular."

"By yourself?"

"Yes," I say, equally passive-aggressive. "I need some *me* time."

Thank goodness our food arrives, and the topic of tomorrow is soon forgotten.

After that, dinner continues with no more incidents. My mom, miraculously, doesn't even mention The Mistake at all. Guess my apologies at least worked on her. For the first time in forever, I'm able to end a meal with my family without feeling like a filthy cockroach who let all of them down. I'm feeling even a little optimistic about the future.

I look up at Archie who's also looking at me. Every time I've gazed in his direction tonight, his eyes have been on me. Is it because of him that I'm feeling this new confidence? Because I've known that no matter what, there'd be someone at the table 100 per cent on my side?

And will I be able to keep believing in myself next week when he'll be gone? Yes, I feel like something in me has healed for good this week, but I'll sure miss his hands, and his mouth, and, yeah, his Princess Sofia. But I'm afraid what I'll miss the most will be his heart, even if it's never been mine.

I finish my wine and put the thought away. We still have three more nights together.

We're waiting for the desserts when Tucker's phone pings. He reads the text, and I swear he blushes.

"Sorry," he says, standing up. "I have to go, there's an emergency with the... uh... flower delivery."

"This late at night?" Mom asks. "What could it possibly be?"

Winter goes into bridezilla mode at once. "Is it serious? Fixable?"

"Yeah, yeah." Tucker waves her off. "Nothing I can't solve with a phone call, but I'd better go now. Can you ask them to put my share of dinner on my room? I'm in 451."

The room next to Archie, I realize with a swallow. I hope the walls are thick.

Dad waves his request down. "Don't be silly, young man, tonight's dinner's on me. And thank you again for all the hard work you've put into organizing the perfect wedding for my daughter."

"No trouble at all, sir. Well, I'll see you all tomorrow."

Tucker says goodbye one last time and walks out of the restaurant, leaving the rest of us to endure at least another hour of chit-chat before we can make our escape.

The bill arrives exactly seventy-five minutes later, not that I'm counting. Dad puts it on his room tab, and we get up to walk toward the elevators. The six of us can all fit inside, so we all go in one trip. Archie and I strategically keep to the back on opposite corners. Thankfully,

Winter and Logan are on the first floor and my parents are on the second.

The moment the elevator doors ding shut after my parents have gone, it's as if someone has shouted, "Ready, steady, go!" Archie and I fly into each other's arms and kiss like two people who've been eye-flirting for the past three and a half hours and can't wait to tear their clothes off.

When the elevator doors swish open, I make to follow Archie outside but bump into a solid wall of muscled back instead.

"What's up?" I ask, peering around his shoulder.

"That sneaky weasel," Archie whispers. "Flower emergency, my ass. Looks like Tucker is banging that actor's assistant. I called it, didn't I?"

"What? Are you sure? How can you tell?"

"They're making out outside his room."

"Let me see." I peek my head forward between the elevator doors, which have already tried to close on us twice.

Down the hall, Penny is leaving Tucker's room, but the goodbye is taking forever. They're kissing on the threshold, making out like a pair of horny teenagers. We can't go into Archie's room with them in the hallway and risk being spotted.

Archie reads my mind, because he asks, "How long do you think that's going to take?"

"Too long," I say, pulling him back inside. "Let's go to my room."

One floor down, we tumble out of the elevator into the hall, which is thankfully clear of people. Giggling like two idiots we kiss and touch all the way along the corridor.

At the door, I fish out the key and try to fit it into the lock while Archie distractingly nibbles at my ear from behind.

"We're never getting in if you keep doing that," I say.

Archie gives me a little space, but as soon as the door is unlocked, he lifts me and carries me to the bed with surprising gentleness for a man so big. He climbs on top of me, pinning my arms above my head, and just hovers above me, looking into my eyes for the longest time. A breath catches in my chest. This feels intense, too intense. So, I chicken out and close my eyes, arching my back and moaning to bring the interaction to a sexual plane.

Sex, I can handle.

Emotions, on the other hand, are running out of my control. Have been since the start.

* * *

A knock at the door wakes me up the next morning. "Sammy, it's me, open up."

Shoot. Winter. What is she doing outside my room? What time is it? I check the alarm clock on the nightstand: 7.00 a.m., pretty early.

Archie groans awake. "What—?"

I place a hand over his mouth. "Shhh. It's my sister."

The knocking turns to pounding. "Sammy. Summer."

Archie picks up the hand covering his mouth, kisses the palm, and lowers it to his chest. "What does she want?" he whispers.

"I don't know."

"Aren't you going to answer?"

"With you here? No way," I hiss. "Winter will think I'm in the shower or something and leave."

Sure enough, after a few more minutes, the attack on the door ends and the hall beyond goes quiet.

I drop back onto the pillow, blowing hair away from my face. "That was close."

I wonder what Winter wanted; I'll have to check on her as soon as the naked evidence of my transgressions is out of my bed.

"Would it be so bad if she found us together?"

I raise onto my elbows. "With everything she told me about you, the way she worries about me, and it being the day before her wedding? Yeah-ha. She'd go nuts!"

Archie puts a hand over his chest in mock pain. "I feel deeply stereo-typed here."

"Poor you." I bend over and kiss him on the forehead. "You want some coffee?"

"Sure."

I slip on my panties and pull the white, long-to-my-knees T-shirt I use as pajamas over my head. The shirt has taken a vacation on this trip so far as I've slept mostly naked... Mmm... I let out a contented sigh and get up. The moment I step into the kitchenette, however, my sense of serene satiation evaporates as the pounding on the door resumes.

"Sammy, Sammy, it's me."

Oh my gosh, is my sister ever going to give up? She's going to wake up the entire floor at this rate. I put a finger to my lips in a shush gesture directed at Archie. If we keep quiet, Winter will have to cease and desist, eventually.

But that hope shatters when I hear a key turning in the lock. How does she have a key to my room?

My chest explodes in a panic, and my heartbeat picks up a frenzied tempo and then decelerates when the door opens barely an inch before the inner bolt stops it with a loud thud. Thank goodness I always put the extra lock on by reflex, even if I don't have a recollection of doing it last night. Apparently old habits can survive even rabid sex exploits.

In a blur, I collect all of Archie's clothes from where they're scattered around the bedroom. Jeans, shoes, and socks on the floor. His sweater from the back of a chair, and his T-shirt draped over the bed's headboard.

"Get up," I hiss, and frantically scan the room to check if I've missed anything.

Meanwhile, my sister is trying to peek her head inside while she keeps calling my name.

When Archie is up, emerging stark naked from under the sheets, I don't even take the time to admire his sculpted body. A clear sign of how agitated I am. I simply force the ball of clothes into his arms and push him into the bathroom, frantically whispering, "Hide in the shower. Pull the curtain."

Then, I rush back into the main room, closing the bathroom door behind me. Hand still on the handle, I take a steadying breath and finally answer my sister.

"I'm coming, I'm coming." I hurry to the door. "Get your head out so I can remove the bolt."

Winter obeys, and I close the door with a soft click, remove the lock, and open the door wide to let her in.

"Oh my gosh!" She barrels into the room. "Are you okay?" Winter grabs my shoulders and pats down my arms as if to check I'm whole.

"Yeah, I am." I shrug free. "What are you doing in my room at seven in the morning? And why do you have a key?"

"You weren't answering, so I went to the reception and pretended to be you to get a duplicate. Why weren't you answering?"

"That's illegal," I say, ignoring the second question.

"Oh, please, as if you've never pretended to be me."

"Not since we were teenagers," I retort pettily. "What's up, did something happen?"

"No, I just wanted to catch you before you disappeared off to yoga, and then... What is it again you're doing today?"

I see my plan of spending the day with Archie exploring Napa together, having lunch in a quiet bistro, and pretending we're a couple evaporate before my eyes once again.

Is it a wise plan? Pretending we're together? Probably not. Do I care? Nu-uh.

And I hate that I have to lie to my sister, but I want one full day with Archie so much. Tomorrow is the day of the wedding, and there won't be any sneaking off then. And tomorrow night will be our last together. I squash the panic rising in my chest at the mere thought.

The bottom line is, I need today. This entire week is about her. And even if we haven't really spent a lot of time together, I deserve a day for myself.

"I told you, nothing in particular. I planned to go exploring a little."

"Yeah, some *me* time you said, right?" She's not buying it.

I'm trying to come up with a believable answer when I spot Archie's boxer briefs peeking out from under the bed, one second before my sister's laser-focused gaze clocks in on them.

"Are those men's underpants?" Winter asks.

In a desperate move, I kick them further under the bed. "No," I say, blushing head to toe.

"You have a man stashed up in here!" My sister smiles. "That's why you didn't come to the door. Why are you hiding him?"

"Please, no one else is here."

Winter's face turns suspicious. "No, seriously, where is he hiding?" Then her gaze narrows. "Who is he?"

"*He* doesn't exist."

"Really?" Winter crosses the space between us. "So, you wouldn't mind if I looked"—with a theatrical gesture, she opens the closet door—"in here!"

Hanging from the rack, only my bridesmaid dress comes into view.

"See?" I say. "No one's here."

Winter still looks unconvinced, but I'm beginning to hope she'll let it go, when the clear sound of a sneeze echoes from the bathroom.

With an a-ha look, my sister marches into the en suite, and, after a few seconds' pause, I hear the shower curtain being yanked open.

"*You*?" Winter gasps.

"Hi, Snowflake," Archie's husky voice replies. "If I said I was here only to take a shower 'cause mine is broken, you wouldn't believe me, would you?"

"I can't believe this!"

Winter marches out of the bathroom and Archie follows her, wearing only his jeans—commando style. He looks deliciously disheveled, like a half-unwrapped candy. And even after the night we've had, I want for my sister to get out of the way so I can have my sugar fix. Not happening. Winter doesn't seem keen on going anywhere, and when her accusatory glare sets on me, I swallow. Oh, gosh.

She turns back to Archie and points an accusing finger at him. Here we go...

"*How could you?*"

Well, that's a little offensive. That she'd direct her rage only at Archie as if I were a gullible idiot who had fallen for his Casanova charm with no clue. There are two of us here, and I can decide for myself.

"Relax, Winter," I say. "Nothing shady is going on. We're two consenting adults who decided to have fun together while at a wedding. No need to go ballistic."

The comment, even if technically accurate, sounds a little empty now. So much has changed from that first night when all I wanted was to forget my name.

My sister turns on me, and I'm not sure if I've been quick enough to hide the uncertainty from my features, because she stares at me with her mouth gaping open, incredulous.

"Having *fun*," she scoffs. "Of course." Then she throws a look at Archie so seething it'd finish melting the Arctic. "Get dressed and come to my room," she orders him. "We need to talk."

"No, you don't," I say. "This is none of your business."

The icecap-melting gaze pivots to me. "This is my wedding," she all but shouts, her voice a few octaves shriller. "*Everything* is my business."

Then she turns on her heel and marches out, calling, "Archibald Hill, get your ass to my room, *now!*" Winter slams the door behind her.

16

ARCHIE

Better dressed—the briefs were a bitch to retrieve from under the bed—but still unshowered, I knock on Winter and Logan's door, ready to have my ass kicked.

When I get in, Logan throws me a "Seriously, man?" *look, with a passive-aggressive postscript of,* "If you had to screw the bride's sister, couldn't you at least not get caught the day before the wedding?"

So, my friend is up to speed on the situation.

On the other side of the room, Winter doesn't spare me a second glance; she's too busy pacing around.

When she stops and turns on me, her features contort in a gut-freezing expression of fury I pray never to witness on Summer's face.

"Explain yourself," Winter demands.

"You want me to give a speech about the birds and the bees or something?"

"Don't you try to be a smartass about this. What do you think you're doing?"

"Listen, you're overreacting... Summer and I, we have an understanding." I ignore the, "No, man, don't even try to go down that road," face Logan is making behind Winter's back and keep going. "All the cards are on the table. We're going to enjoy each other's company while we're here, and then go our separate ways at the end of the week."

That doesn't sound as right as it did a few days ago, but the logistics of our future is something Summer and I will have to figure out later, *on our own.* Her sister doesn't get a say.

Winter has a different opinion on the matter. "Unbelievable. What are you, bridesmaid and best man with benefits?"

"If you had to put a label on it, sure."

"My sister doesn't do casual sex."

I'm about to say she's pretty spectacular at it, when Logan's, "Don't you dare," silent warning stops me, and I purse my lips.

"Why are you so mad, exactly?" I ask.

"Because you're taking advantage of my sister."

"I've been clear from the start what this was—"

"Please, don't give me *any* of that crap. You knew she was lonely and vulnerable and you used it to get laid. How long has it been going on?" Winter points an accusing finger at me. "I told you that first morning at breakfast that my sister was off-limits."

I shrug. "Well, sorry, you were exactly one night too late."

Her jaw drops. "What? How? You were late on Monday; when did you find the time? You... you what? Walked into the lobby and, five minutes later, my sister was warming your bed?"

"We had dinner at the same bar and we bonded over a game of hockey."

"You mean you seduced her."

I don't answer.

"Oh my gosh! So, you've been sneaking around behind everyone's backs since we got here?"

Still, I don't speak.

"Every night?"

And a few afternoons, too. I muse while keeping my mouth firmly shut.

Now she turns to Logan. "Say something. He's your best man!"

My friend shrugs. "I can't control what he does, and neither can you."

"Of course you'd be on his side," Winter snaps.

I'd hardly call that having my back, but I can see why Logan needs to keep neutral.

"Listen, Snowflake, I promise no one is getting hurt here."

"Don't you dare 'Snowflake' me. And are you really so dumb to think Summer won't be crushed when you ride away into the sunset alone on Sunday night?"

"That was the initial plan, but nothing has to end on Sunday. Not that it's any of your business."

"Great! So, you're ready to have a girlfriend? A relationship? With my sister?"

"Maybe, I don't know. Do I have to decide now?"

Winter's eyes narrow to slits. "Before you lead her on some more, *yes*."

"I'm not leading anyone on, I've always been honest about where I stood."

"And where do you stand exactly?" The bride-to-be crosses her arms over her chest and taps her foot on the floor, positively livid. "Let's say you're ready for long-distance monogamy. Hard to believe, but anyway. What would you want out of this hypothetical relationship? A family, marriage, kids?"

"I've only known your sister for four days; I don't think kids should be on the table for now, and I sure as hell shouldn't be discussing it with you."

"Not on the table *for now* you say, huh? What about for later?"

"What do you want me to say?"

"Do you want kids, like ever, yes or no?"

I look at her, taken aback.

"That's not a hard question," she insists. "You should already know the answer. And you should definitely know the answer before you even consider a relationship with Summer."

"Why?"

Winter walks toward me, stopping a mere foot away. She's shorter than me, but somehow manages to look down her nose at me. "Care to know where Summer was just a few weeks ago?"

"Uh...?"

"She was in New York, freezing her eggs. *Comprende?*"

I squint. What is she talking about?

The rant continues. "You know why? Because Summer is the kind of woman who wants to get married and have a family so bad, she was willing to put herself through weeks of medical exams and hormone shots to secure that future. And not just *any* family. She wants a big one. A soccer team of cute, chubby babies squealing around the house. So, tell me again, how many kids do you want?"

Honestly, I don't know if I see myself as a father. And definitely not in the immediate future.

Winter must read the answer on my silent features, because next, she says, "That's what I thought." She comes an inch closer and hisses, "Do me a favor next time you're"—she makes air quotes—"'having fun with my sister'. Take a good look at how she stares at you, and then tell me again how no one is going to get hurt."

* * *

Winter's words stay with me long after I leave her room. Does she have a point? Are Summer and I not right for each other? Our chemistry is amazing, and I always have fun when I'm with her, but it's true we haven't discussed any of the more serious topics. Because that's not what people who plan to have a week-long fling do. But I won't lie: being with her hasn't felt like a casual fling past that first night together.

Let's take a look at the hard facts.

I don't want to say goodbye to Summer come Sunday. But I also never saw myself as the getting married or having kids type.

My entire life has been a no-strings gig. Hop on a plane to Africa today, and leave for South America next month. I've never been tied down to a particular place or to a person. I've never seen the point. And I've never wanted to settle down or even been tempted to—until now?

But with Summer... well, let's say the idea of coming home to her every night wouldn't be that horrible. But do screaming goblins have to be part of the deal?

And does that make Summer and I as incompatible as Winter claims? We can't be, not when we fit so well together.

Summer is the first woman who's stirred in me something other than lust, something deeper.

But frozen-eggs deep?

17

SUMMER

Two hours and Archie still hasn't returned. What did my sister say to him? I'm still too mad at Winter to call her and ask. But why is it taking so long? Are our plans for today still on?

I check my phone for the hundredth time; the screen remains black. Like a watched pot, it won't ring, ping, vibrate... nothing.

To kill time, I've showered and tried out at least a million outfits before settling on light-washed jeans and a simple T-shirt, with my comfortable-to-walk-in-but-pretty, tie-up wedges.

How long should I wait? Should I call—

A knock on the door puts an end to the self-doubting. I run to open and then chide myself in a *be-cool* way, slow down to a walk, and wait a respectable number of heartbeats before I throw the door ajar.

Archie is standing on the other side, gloriously hot in dark jeans and a white T-shirt so tight he could be bare-chested. The hair at his nape is still damp, meaning he must've just gotten out of the shower. If I had to assign him a fantasy today, he'd be the sweaty window washer man from that old Diet Coke commercial.

"Hey," I say. "You're alive." I step aside to let him in, and then close the door behind him. "How did the telling-off go?"

He's staring out of the window and has avoided meeting my gaze since he walked in.

"Apparently, I'm not allowed to date you."

Date me? I try not to dwell on the label or read too much into it. He's probably trying to find a classier way of saying, *"I'm not allowed to have sex with you and then dump you at the end of the week."*

No, that's not fair. It was mutually agreed this fling would have an expiration date, and I can't get mad at him for sticking to the plan. I won't be one of those women who say it's okay to have a casual relationship and then ask for a ring within a week.

A nervous chuckle croaks up my throat. "I'm an adult, you know. I don't need my sister's permission to do anything."

"Right," he says. "Sorry I didn't come to yoga."

Oh, guess our big, *"Where is this going?"* talk is over. I recover quickly from the disappointment and follow his lead, saying, "No, don't worry. I didn't go either."

A lie.

I dressed up and waited downstairs at the resort's entrance to see if he'd show up. When he didn't, I trekked back to my room, tail between my legs. And not because I couldn't go to a yoga class on my own; I skipped it to do the rest of the class a favor. Those folks have been doing Acro practice in couples for the best part of a week, and I didn't want to ruin the last lesson for everyone else with my odd number status. A pity, since there are no classes on the weekend, and this would've been our last Acro Yoga class together... forever?

And there I go again, wondering about a future that involves him.

Archie is silent and a little disconnected, so I ask, "You still want to go to that brewery?"

"Sure," he says. "You have a jacket?"

I don't understand the question. Or rather, I get its literal meaning, but not its point. "Yeah, why?"

I grab my gray suede jacket from the closet, which I brought in case the nights became chilly.

"Want to go on the bike?" Archie asks. "I have an extra helmet."

Is this something he does with all his flings? Take them on his bike for a last ride into the sunset before he says goodbye? How many women have been in my position before?

I shake the image away and refrain from asking how many ladies have donned that same headgear. If people had to be judged only by their past, where would that put me?

The bike is everything I expected: big, black, and sleek. But seeing Archie zip up his black leather jacket, don his helmet, and mount his ride, it's not something I'm prepared for. Watching him rev the bike gets me all hot and bothered, prompting the usual flutters in my belly I can't control. And thuds in my chest I can't control. And I might've drooled if I hadn't swallowed in quick succession a couple of times. This man is hitting all my emotional and lust buttons simultaneously.

The coup de grâce comes when Archie grins at me, the first real smile since he came back from seeing my sister. "Ready?"

The sun is bouncing off his black helmet and motorcycle bodywork, and he has never been more of a forbidden fruit I crave with all my being. With a sinking heart, I realize I do want him to be mine. I want to see that smile every day, while the reality of our situation couldn't be further away from this fantasy.

The grin drops from his face as he stares up at me. "Are you scared?"

"Yes," I say.

Only not about the bike, I add in my head.

"Don't be," Archie says, an incredible tenderness lacing his tone as he extends a hand toward me. "I've got you."

I take his hand and mount behind him. In for a penny, in for a pound. I mean, at this point, the pain of letting him go will be the same no matter what I do in the next few days, so I might as well enjoy the time we have left together before I retire to a convent and really go off men for the rest of my life.

The rumble of the bike underneath my thighs shakes me away from any wishful thinking, grounding me in the present. The second he twists the accelerator, I gladly take the excuse to wrap my arms around his waist and hold on as tightly as I can. His back is broad and hard and warm, and I want to keep hugging him like a baby koala for the rest of my life.

We exit the resort at walking speed, but once we're on the open road,

Archie opens the gas, and the engine roars in response, tires skidding on the concrete. The bike's rumble is powerful; maybe too loud, too in your face, just like its owner, and I love it. I love the vibrations crawling up from my legs to my upper body. I love the speed. The sensation of flying. And I'm afraid I might be a tiny bit in love with the driver as well.

A steep turn in the road makes my stomach drop and my focus shift as Archie bends the bike closer to the ground, then straightens it up again in a split second. I close my eyes, tightening my embrace, and hope this ride will never end.

Archie works the clutch, making the bike gather even more speed, again giving me the perfect excuse to tighten my grip on his waist. In response, one of Archie's hands moves onto mine and gives a gentle squeeze before he has to get it back on the handle. A small gesture, but one that makes my chest swell with opposite sensations: warmth and sadness. Wonder, at how attentive this man can be. How sweet. While also being hot and manly and a bad biker boy. And hopelessness, at the waste of him refusing any long-term attachment. Archie would be an amazing partner, if only he gave it a chance... And, oh my gosh, here I go again, trying to turn him into something he's not. Wanting to mold him to my expectations, when he's a free agent and has never claimed any different.

Summer, I give myself another pep talk, you gotta live in the moment, girl. 'Cause that's all you're gonna get.

I must focus on enjoying the ride. The intimacy the bike affords us. Physical, for how close our bodies are, and emotional, for the trust I have to put in him, surrendering all control. That's how it's been with Archie from the start. I might've set some stupid rules, but he's been the one in charge since he promised to make me forget my name that first night.

The plan succeeded. But at what price? What will it take to forget *him?*

Green country sweeps by, and I wish we could exist in this suspended universe forever, where there's only him and me on a bike. Our bodies so close they might've been fused. My heart is pounding faster and faster, jacked up on adrenaline at every turn, incline, and acceleration Archie makes. If this is what flying feels like, I wish humans were born with wings.

But all too soon, we reach our destination. Archie parks in the brewery parking lot, and I let go of his chest as fast as if I'd been electrocuted. The daydream is over; now we're back to reality, to a world where in two days we'll say goodbye to each other for good. I'd better remember that and keep reminding myself: enjoy the time you have left, but start distancing yourself.

I hop off the bike and begin the act. Like a person without a care in the world, I unhook my helmet and hand it to him, saying, "That was amazing."

Archie smiles, removing his helmet. And I have to suppress the instinct to run my fingers through his hair to flatten it out. Right now it's deliciously disheveled, sticking out in all directions.

"You were a dream passenger," Archie says, after securing both helmets to the bike. He comes close to me and pokes my nose. "Not a wobble in you."

Ah, because he has no idea how precarious my knees feel right now. Wobbly doesn't begin to cover it.

He raises a bent elbow, offering it to me. "Shall we?"

I nod, link our arms, and we head inside the brewery.

The visit, and the two pints of beer, relax the tension between us. But at lunch, Archie spaces out again. His attention seems to be focused elsewhere—a million miles away from our conversation. That is when there's any talking happening at all and we're not trapped in long, uncomfortable silences. I do my best to keep chatting, but whenever I ask him questions, Archie's responses consist of one-word yes and no answers. And he never has any questions for me. Once we've made our order—we're in a French bistro in Yountville—I can't take the weirdness any longer and finally ask, "Are you sure you're okay? Did something my sister tell you freak you out?"

Archie stares at me. And his gaze is present and not the least detached when he asks, "Did you really freeze your eggs?"

18

SUMMER

I'm going to kill my sister. Strangle her. Drown her in confetti.

I want the ground to open and swallow me whole. Or, better, I want a meteor to fall from the sky and obliterate us. I wish lightning would strike our table, even if we're sitting under a porch and it's not even raining. Or for the San Andreas fault to finally get a move on and bring The Big One. Because anything, *anything* would be better than having to answer this question.

I cover my face with my hands and peek at him from between my fingers. "I can't believe she told you that."

Archie makes a charming frown, a cross between amusement and embarrassment. Then he reaches for my hands and gently lowers them to the table. "Why? It isn't a bad thing."

"It's very personal," I say. "Why did you bring it up?"

Archie sighs. "These last few days... we had fun, didn't we?"

Fun isn't supposed to be a negative word, but I'm seriously starting to despise it. What does *fun* mean in his head? The constant uncertainty makes me snap, "Yeah, a blast. Only two days left; we'd better enjoy ourselves."

I take a long sip of wine.

"That's not what I meant," Archie says. I can tell he's struggling to find the right words. "What I wanted to say is that I've enjoyed being with you..." Loaded pause. "Honestly, more than I've enjoyed being with anyone else in the past." I hate my heart for the leap it does in my chest. "And I was wondering if we could... maybe... uhm... see each other even after the wedding is over." My treacherous heart keeps soaring into the air. "But then your sister..."

My heart is at that point in mid-air where it has to come down from its jump, and Archie's last comment makes it lose focus and balance, and the poor organ ends up going down in an uncontrolled spin until it splatters on the floor of my rib cage.

"But then my sister brought frozen eggs into the picture, and it all became a bit much?" I suggest.

"Yeah, I mean, no. Not exactly. What do the frozen eggs mean? If it's okay for me to ask. You don't have to answer if you don't want to."

Too late for that. My sister put all my cards on the table, so I might as well play my hand. I look at him and try really hard not to picture what a fantastic sperm donor he'd be, how beautiful our babies would look.

I go with a casual answer, trying to lighten the mood. "I won't go into technical details, but the gist of it is that after thirty-five a woman's fertility drops—"

An embarrassed cough behind me makes me stop. A server is hovering next to our table with two plates in his hands. I lean back in my chair and give him space to set the appetizers down. He does, and once he's at a safe distance, I don't even pretend I'm interested in my food.

"In short," I continue, "I'm cheating biology to give myself more time to have kids."

"More time." Archie looks like he's digesting this information. He picks up his fork and moves Brussels sprouts around on his plate. "But you definitely want kids?"

"Not tomorrow, but one day, yeah, I want to have kids."

"And to get married."

Gosh, my sister really put the heavy load on him.

"Yes," I say, working hard not to grit my teeth. He's making marriage and kids sound like dirty words or something. "If I were in a relationship, it would have to be with someone who's on the same page about having a family, eventually. I'm in no rush, but that's the end goal for me."

Archie looks up at me, a death sentence in his eyes. "I don't know if I want kids. Up until a few days ago, I'd never even considered the possibility of settling down with someone. My job requires me to travel a lot and I wouldn't even know if all that traveling would be compatible with a family."

"Isn't Logan's job the same? He's marrying my sister."

"Yeah, but he's cutting down on the traveling and I'm not sure if that's what I want. I'm not Logan."

"No one asked you to be."

Archie passes a hand down his face. "Summer, let's be honest with each other like we've been from day one. Are kids and marriage a deal breaker for you?"

I could lie, I could say no. I could spend the next however many years of my life loving this man and being happy. But how long before I resented him? How long before I blamed him for not having the family I've always dreamt of? If the past year has taught me something, it is that lying to myself is pointless.

I look him in the eyes and nod. "Yes, one day, I want to have a family. Are kids a deal breaker for you?"

His face remains stony, and he doesn't respond.

And there it is, the ugly truth my sister has forced us to reveal to each other sooner rather than later. The San Andreas fault might as well have opened in the middle of our table, putting us on separate ridges, because we've never been so far apart.

"Okay," I say, swallowing a glob of sorrow. Then I shrug in a "So what?" way. "Guess we'll have to stick to the plan, then, and say goodbye on Sunday."

Archie's eyes cloud over, and the lines on his forehead crease further as he remains in a stony silence.

I've lost all my appetite, and the idea of riding back to the resort on Archie's bike makes my stomach churn even more. I throw my napkin on the table and get up, saying, "I need to use the restroom."

Instead, I walk out of the restaurant and call a cab. Once I'm safely inside and out of Archie's reach, I text him.

TO ARCHIE

> Sorry, I couldn't stay

> This was a mistake

Archie doesn't text back.

* * *

I spend half the afternoon crying while taking a bath, and the other half crying while watching a marathon of *One Tree Hill* on TV. The teen show with its high emotions helps me mourn my own love story that will never be.

I want to be with Archie; every fiber in my body yearns for it.

But he's not relationship material.

No, that's not true or fair. The only problem here is that the man isn't playing for keeps, because if he were, he'd be a fantastic boyfriend, husband, and father. Archie is kind and attentive when the situation calls for it, but also knows how to lighten the mood with a joke when things aren't that serious. He has had many women, but I bet that if he picked one as his forever and ever, he'd be loyal till the end of times. As a partner, he'd be solid, generous, reassuring, frigging hot, fun to be with, interesting, challenging, protective but not asphyxiating, full of life, and amazing in bed.

And I can also picture him being an amazing dad so clearly, it hurts. He'd be his kids' hero. Being the kind of dad who builds a treehouse in our backyard. Because we'd be the kind of family with the white-fenced house, the cat, and three kids, two boys and a girl.

And I've crashed into fantasyland again. I'd better rein in my imagination. No part of this dream of mine will ever happen. Maybe five, or ten, years from now when he could be ready or open to the idea of kids. But that's a big if. I can't spend years with a guy, hoping one day he'll change his mind about having a family. If he'd said, yeah, I want kids, just not right now, I could've said yippee ki yay frozen eggs, we have all the time in the world.

But he didn't, and I can't dive head-first into another relationship that I know will end in a total disaster.

We're doomed.

Story of my life.

I hate it.

19

SUMMER

Tomorrow's lunch will be held on the beautiful lawn behind the estate, but tonight it's too cold to dine outside, so the rehearsal dinner has been moved indoors.

Standing signs engraved with *Spencer & Knowles Rehearsal Dinner* point to a spacious room I haven't seen yet. This must be the space the resort uses for indoor receptions when it rains or is too cold. The salon is next to the breakfast hall and mirrors it, two halves of the same pie. A nice choice for indoor events. The faraway glass wall provides a beautiful view of the lit vineyards even at night, and the outside patio is decorated with strung fairy lights, adding even more romance to the atmosphere. The only thing I wouldn't necessarily like for a wedding is the carpeted floor. Its intricate leaves and flower pattern are not bad per se, but they're a strong reminder we're in a hotel and not a magical place lost in a fable world somewhere.

I'm so absorbed in my observations, I don't notice Archie coming my way until he's standing right in front of me.

"Can we talk?" he asks.

I'm not ready for the ambush, and I'm tempted to flee again but can't see a way out. Instead, I use attack as the best defense.

"There's nothing left to say."

His eyes widen. "Are you mad at me?"

"Yes, I'm mad at you and I'm mad at myself. I don't want to talk to you, especially not where everybody can hear."

Archie purses his lips. "Let's move somewhere else, then, but we're going to talk *now*."

I oblige him, mostly because other guests are streaming into the room and I want to avoid making a scene.

He pushes the patio doors open and I follow him outside. Luckily, the rehearsal dinner is due to start in less than ten minutes. As excruciating as this heart-to-heart will turn out, at least it'll be short.

We walk away from the French windows so the people inside won't be able to spot us, and, as soon as we turn the corner, Archie crowds my personal space. "Explain to me how, in this scenario, *you* get to be mad at me."

"You didn't text me back," I reply, irrationally mad.

"I didn't text—" He scoffs, and shakes his head. "You left me in a restaurant mid-meal, making me look like a complete ass."

Is that what he cares about?

"Sorry if I embarrassed you. Don't go back to that restaurant and you'll be fine."

"I don't give a damn about the restaurant people. You walked out on me," he accuses.

True, I did, but... I say the next part aloud. "Sorry, but I couldn't sit there and listen to you tell me how this is never going to work. How we're never going to happen. I just couldn't."

"Yeah? And what would a text have solved?"

"Nothing, you're right. This situation is unsolvable. But don't worry, come Sunday, you'll be free to go back to banging an endless stream of women. Hell, you can start tonight for all I care."

I make to walk away, but Archie gently grabs me by the elbow. "Don't walk away again." The phrase comes out as half a plea and half an order.

I yank my arm free. "Why? You've made it clear where you stand."

"Really? Because I've no idea myself. Why don't you explain it to me?"

I turn back to him, the irrational rage of a few seconds ago gone. It's sheer pain that makes my breath shallow as I speak next. "If this thing between us were to move past Sunday, I want commitment, a future.

Marriage, family, kids. And you can't give me any of those things right now. And I'd be okay waiting if all it took was time, but I'm not sure you'll ever want the same things I do. So what's the point?" The question comes out in half a sob. "We're like a square peg and a round hole. No matter how hard we try, we'll never fit together."

Archie stares at me, at a loss for words. I want him to deny it. To say I'm wrong. That we can be together. But his mouth stays inexorably shut while his eyes search mine in a panic. Whether it's fear of losing me or of being tied down to me forever, I can't say. And I've had to deal with too many shitty situations in my life to follow another unicorn. I can't force him to want something he doesn't.

So, I walk away.

This time, he lets me.

* * *

Throughout the entire rehearsal dinner, I keep my head down and push the food around on my plate without trying more than a few bites. My wine glass, on the other hand, empties and gets refilled much quicker, so that by the time the dessert arrives, I'm very tipsy. In my alcohol-induced semi-euphoria, I stop seeing why being with Archie would be wrong. Suddenly, the prospect of having sex with him tonight becomes much more attractive. So, when everybody begins to mingle and walk around the room, I get up as well, bringing my unfinished glass of wine with me. I wait for Archie to be alone by the pastry station—there's a mini-desserts and fruit buffet—to saunter up to him.

"My room or yours?" I slur.

His eyes widen. "What?"

"I want to have sex. Should we do it in your room or mine?"

Archie frowns at the glass in my hands. "How much have you had to drink?"

I shrug. "A few glasses."

"You're drunk."

"Am not. I want sex."

"You're in no position to make that decision tonight."

"Want to discuss positions? Okay, I'm game. Up for something we haven't tried yet?"

"I'm taking you to bed."

I roll my eyes. "Finally."

Archie tries to take the glass from me, but I snatch my hand away before he can grab it. The red liquid inside sloshes dangerously close to the rim, but stays in—mostly. I watch, mesmerized, as a few droplets fly out and land on the carpet, disappearing into the intricate pattern.

"What's happening here?"

I look up from the floor to find my sister standing next to us, a fake, let's-keep-up-appearances smile plastered on her lips.

"She's drunk," Archie says, just as I say, "We were about to go have sex."

All pretend politeness washes out of my sister's face as she glares at Archie. "You wouldn't—"

He stops her before she can continue. "No, exactly, I wouldn't. I'm taking your sister to her room *to sleep*. And that's it. You know me better than that."

Winter gives him another hard, this-is-all-your-fault stare, but nods.

While I'm distracted, Archie successfully removes the glass from my hands and steers me toward the exit door.

I turn my head over my shoulder and wave at my sister. "Nighty, nighty."

In my room, Archie undresses me until I'm stripped down to my underwear. I try to kiss him, but he fends off my attacks, his superior height proving determinant.

Then he picks me up as easily as if I were a child and deposits me into bed, tucking me under the covers. I tap the space next to me in what I hope is a seductive move.

Before he obliges me, Archie brings me a glass of water. He looks so broody, I drink like a good girl. He takes the empty glass from me and sits on the bed, but dressed and above the sheets, I note.

Still, this position allows me to hug him.

"Come on," I say, wrapping my arms around his torso. "What are you waiting for? I want sex."

"No, you don't, trust me."

I'm so tired of people telling me what I should and shouldn't want, should or shouldn't do. "And you're a coward. Too much of a chicken to risk caring about someone other than yourself."

"On that, you might be right, baby." He drops a kiss on my forehead. "I'm scared."

"Don't call me baby." I punch his chest, trying to pull back, but he keeps me in place with my face resting on his stupidly hard chest. "I'm not your baby. You hate babies. You're a big, Viking, baby hater."

"You're tired," he murmurs in a soft voice, stroking my hair and ignoring my ramblings.

"I'm not," I reply, even as a treacherous yawn escapes my lips.

Archie's chest is moving in a rhythmic, soothing motion underneath me, and his hand is working magic on my scalp. Gradually, my eyelids begin to droop, and I close them just for a second... I only need to rest for a moment, and then we... I never finish that thought as sleep takes me over.

20

SUMMER

The next morning, I wake up with the shrill sound of the room telephone piercing my eardrums. I roll over and scramble to grab the receiver.

"Hello?"

"Good morning, Miss Knowles," a polite female voice says. "This is your wake-up call."

"I didn't set up a wake-up call."

"Oh, I'm so sorry, Miss Knowles. Let me check our records." After a brief pause, the woman talks again. "It shows here your sister requested the call."

"Okay, thank you."

"She's also asked us to remind you that you're expected in the bridal suite in an hour for hair and makeup."

"Thank you." I slam the receiver down and collapse back on the pillow.

I'm alone in bed. Archie must've snuck out after he put me to sleep. A small pounding picks up in my chest as I think about what a fool I made of myself last night. But the emotional cringe has nothing on the pounding in my skull.

Damn. A headache is splitting my head in two. My eyeballs feel as heavy as lead in their sockets. And a queasiness infests my stomach. The famous oath every hungover person swears pops into mind: *I'm never going to drink again.*

Of all the days I could get myself into this situation I chose today, the day of the ceremony. When I can't sneak away and hide in a hole. No, I have to stand up at the altar, carry out all my bridesmaid duties, and do it all with a smile on my face.

But for Winter, I can do it. If the months since The Mistake have taught me anything, it's how to function like a normal, semi-happy human being while dying on the inside. So, let's move into hangover survival mode.

First, I open my suitcase to fish out my eye cooling mask and stick it in the minuscule freezing compartment of the minibar.

Next, I survey the drink offerings. I was aiming for water, but I whoop in delight when I see the fridge is supplied with two Gatorades. I guess that, being in Napa, hangovers come with the territory and the hotel has smartly stashed its minibars with electrolyte-rich drinks. I grab both bottles and close the minibar. The choice is between Lemon-Lime and Strawberry. I open the Lemon-Lime, draining all twelve fluid ounces in a few long gulps. I also pop a Tylenol.

The Strawberry I carry with me to the bathroom. I take a quick shower but still apply a generous dose of conditioner to my hair. The blowout and styling will be handled by a professional, but I can't show up with a tangled mess for the hairstylist to sort. Wrapped in a towel, I open and finish the second bottle of Gatorade. Already I'm less queasy, and even if the electrolytes urban legend is bullshit, drinking so many liquids will surely drain the toxins from my body.

I need one last restoration elixir. I walk back to the kitchenette, leaving wet footprints on the floor, and make coffee. For breakfast, I eat a packet of chocolate chip cookies. No way I'm showing my face downstairs before I absolutely have to.

With caffeine and food in my system, I feel better. I check the time on my phone. I still have half an hour before I have to be in the bridal suite, so I set an alarm for twenty-five minutes and go lie on the bed with my now-cool gel mask over my eyes. I let my towel-wrapped head sink into the pillow while the gel massage beads inside the mask work their magic.

By the time the timer goes off, I've fallen asleep again. But it's fine; even this brief nap has done miracles to clear my head. When I walk out of my room, carrying my bridesmaid dress and shoes over my shoulder, I'm in decent, presentable shape, if not at 100 per cent yet.

My sister doesn't seem as proud of my appearance. Winter barely lets me take three steps into the bridal suite before she greets me with the sweetest passive-aggressive smile. "Slept well?"

"Like a baby," I reply, equally catty but polite. "You?"

"Great." She winces and looks away, but she might've shown me her tongue for how mature this conversation has been.

I hang my dress on a hook by the door and take in the room. The walls are covered in a rose and cream floral wallpaper, and the furniture—two armchairs, a couch, and a changing screen—is all in the same print as the walls.

A bit matchy-matchy.

The only break from the blossomy overload is the far end wall, where the wallpaper is covered by three large head-to-torso mirrors, each dotted with lights overhead, like in a theater dressing room. One of them frames the reflection of my irritated sister.

Winter is boiling to say something else, but she's thwarted by the hair-stylist and makeup artist, who get up from the couch and start to divide and conquer. The bride should be the first to have her hair done and the last to put makeup on. The pecking order is bride, maid of honor, simple bridesmaid—aka me—and then the mother of the bride.

Lana and my mother are also here, but so far, except for a genuinely friendly "hello," and "morning, dear," they've kept quiet about last night. Did they even notice the drama? Or did Winter manage to swoop the dust, aka me, under the carpet before anyone noticed I was drunk?

According to the pampering line, Mom and Winter sit in front of the mirrors to get their hair and makeup done, respectively. Since I'll be third to have my hair done and second for the makeup, I can safely assume I have a good half an hour during which I needn't be here. But how can I get away?

"Does anyone want coffee?" I ask.

"Oh, darling." The hairstylist catches my gaze in the mirror. "You don't want a dark, stainy liquid near the bridal gown or bridesmaids' dresses. You wouldn't believe the disasters I've witnessed in my career. Better steer clear of food and drinks."

I nod and refrain from commenting that both the bridal gown and bridesmaids' dresses are safely wrapped in cellophane.

For lack of better alternatives, I sit on the free armchair next to the one occupied by Lana, grab a magazine from the round coffee table between the chairs, and pretend to read. Right now, I can't even make sense of the pictures.

"I saw you were a little upset last night," Lana whispers. "Was it because of Archie?"

I look up from the magazine. "Was I that obvious?"

"Not to anyone else, no, but I can tell when you're tipsy."

Tipsy doesn't exactly cover it. I nod.

"If it helps," Lana keeps talking in hushed tones, "I think he really likes you."

"Of course he likes her," my sister—who must've developed vampire hearing overnight—snaps. "What's not to like?"

"Be careful, dear," the hairstylist interjects. "You don't want me to burn you with a curling iron. Try to keep still."

Unmoving, but just as antagonizing, my sister continues, "The problem is not *if* he likes her, but for *how long*."

"Man, thanks," I snort. "Because it'd be impossible for someone to like me for more than a week."

"It's not you, *it's him!*"

"Girls," my mother cuts into the conversation, "what are you talking about?"

Winter crosses her arms over her chest and pouts like a petulant child. "Ask her."

My mom dodges the makeup artist's brush and turns toward me. "What did you do this time?"

I slam the magazine I was fake reading onto the coffee table with such force I might've dented the wood. "What the hell!" I yell, standing up. "I've made one mistake in my life. *One*. And the only person who could still be cross with me is here"—I point at Lana—"and she's let it go. So why can't you all?"

"Sweetheart, I only asked why your sister was mad at you."

"No, you said, 'What did you do this time?' like it's a regular thing for me to mess up."

"Maybe you're a little too sensitive, dear."

"Because you've made me too sensitive with your constant shows of disappointment." I point at my mother and sister in the mirror. "Both of you." Then, focusing on Winter, I add, "What I do in my free time is none of your business."

"It is when your recreational activities will leave your heart shattered into a million tiny pieces"—she points at her chest—"*I* will have to pick up."

"Don't worry, my heart is not your responsibility."

At this point both the makeup artist and hairstylist have stopped working; my mom and sister are gesticulating too much for them to do anything. Mom turns her chair around and looks up at me. "I still don't understand what's going on?"

"She's sleeping with the best man," Winter rats me out.

Mom looks between us. "That nice fella we met at dinner the other night? What's the issue? Is he single?"

And I swear I want to tear my hair from my head. "Yeah, he's single, Mom; I don't specifically target men in relationships as my dates. This is exactly the behavior I was talking about. One mistake, and you always assume the worst about me. No matter what I do, there'll never be redemption for me. Why can't you just cut me a break?"

Then to myself, I add, *Why do I always have to be the screw-up or the unwanted one? Why can't I just be the happy one for a change?*

"I don't understand." My mother is boiling like a pot in her chair. "If he's single, what's the problem?" This question, at least, is not addressed to me.

"Archibald Hill isn't right for her," Winter says. And the condescension in her tone blows my fuse for good.

I'm about to start yelling again when my mother speaks, and I'm as surprised as my sister when my mom replies, "Well, honey, that's not for you to say." Then she turns to me. "Darling, I'm sorry for jumping to conclusions, I am really. It's just that I hate to see one of my babies suffer. And you, well you haven't been the same since... anyway... I just want you to know we all love you and we want you to be happy and we'll be there for you whatever happens."

The words leave me a little choked, but Winter makes sure to turn the switch back to mad right away.

"Mom, don't encourage her. He's not a smart choice, full stop."

"Oh, because you're the *queen* of smart choices," I yell. "Should I remind you how we got here?"

"What do you mean *here?*"

"With you in a wedding gown."

By this point, I swear the hairstylist is reconsidering her policy of no food and drinks, and would gladly grab a box of popcorn and a Coke.

"What's wrong with me getting married?" Winter accuses.

"Nothing, but let's see all the *smart choices* that brought you to this point..." I tap my chin. "First, you accepted an assignment in a wild, unexplored land with a team you knew nothing about, then got yourself chased through the jungle by maniacs, and shot at, and almost killed. At which point you decided it'd be an excellent idea to sleep with your boss, who, FYI, you hated until the day before, and, tah-dah, a year later you're getting married. You're not smart, you're—"

"What?" my sister yells.

The fight dies out of me, and I sag back on the armchair. "Lucky," I whisper. "You're lucky it all worked out for you. And I'm happy it did. I genuinely am. But this week has been hard for me. Half the people here hate me. And I wanted an escape."

"And you chose the worst possible one." Winter's features soften as well. "Can't you see I just worry about you?"

"Well, you don't have to. Archie has been just a shot of morphine to get me through the week, nothing more. And it will be over by tomorrow, anyway. Or better still, it's already over."

"I'm sorry, Sammy, but it's not that simple."

"Why not?"

"Because there's a problem that comes with using morphine."

"Yeah? Like what?"

"It's addictive."

21

ARCHIE

Like a caged lion, I pace around the groom's suite, brooding about last night. I try to break down my feelings about this quicksand I'm stuck in because I've no clue how to get out, or even if I want an out at all. I've always been so sure. Always so ready to walk away. But with Summer, it's different.

Yeah? How?

My bed was empty last night, and I hated it. No matter that Summer was too drunk to make any conscious decision or stay awake for more than ten minutes, I didn't want to leave her alone, even if it was the right thing to do. I wanted to stay by her side. To hold her. To wake up with the coconutty smell of her hair in my nostrils. To bring her water and an aspirin for the headache she'll be nursing right now. I hate even more that I don't know how she is. And most of all, what she's thinking.

But I also have to face other realities. She's only had wrong relationships in her life, and I can't steal more time from her if I'm not positive I want the same future she does: marriage, kids, to build a family.

Do I want any of those things?

Until a week ago, I would've laughed in anyone's face who suggested it because the idea of settling down, of being tied to one place and one person, always seemed suffocating. But now, I'm not so sure anymore.

Spending every day of the rest of my life with Summer doesn't sound like a prison sentence. In a pre-Summer world, *tying the knot* literally translated for me to putting a length of rope around my neck and jumping. Whereas now, *letting her go* sounds like suicide.

But kids?

Having a baby is not a decision I can change my mind about later, and I'm not sure where I stand.

I wish I could get some fresh air, but, apparently, it's unthinkable for the best man to abandon the groom. As second-in-command, it is my sacred duty to stay put for the next two hours with nothing to do but stare at the walls. Of my two cellmates, the groom seems the most relaxed. Logan is lounging in an armchair, reading a book—he had the sense to bring some entertainment—and looking as if he doesn't have a care in the world. Tucker, on the other end, is sitting straight-backed on the couch, hands resting on his legs, knees bouncing up and down in a nervous rhythm.

What does *he* have to be nervous about?

I can't stand the cabin fever any longer, so I open a window to at least let in some air. Then I sit on one of the revolving chairs in front of the mirrors lining the back wall and spin around a few times. Neither gesture helps to clear my head. Maybe talking would be a better approach.

"Hey, Logie Bear," I say, distracting the groom from his reading.

"Yeah?" My best friend lifts his gaze from his book.

"You think you and Winter will have kids soon?"

Logan shifts a bookmark to the right page, closes the book, and puts it to rest on his lap. "We decided it'd be better to wait until the work in Thailand is over. I wouldn't want to travel so much when they were little."

"But that shouldn't take too long to wrap," I say.

"No, exactly. And now that she's cut back on wild photography expeditions and has her teaching job at the Academy of Art University in San Francisco, we're in a good place to have kids."

"Kids, plural?"

Logan puts the most annoying, dreamy smile on his face. "Yes, we want at least two."

"And was she okay sacrificing her professional life to have a family?"

"She was tired of all the traveling and wanted to put down roots. And we both agreed it'd be better to raise our kids in a smaller town so that's why she's moved to Berkley and I didn't go to LA. But if a great opportunity came along, she could always take the job and leave the kids with me. Her assignments are usually one or two weeks tops." He frowns now. "Well, not leave them as newborns, I suppose, when she was still breast-feeding and stuff, but later, why not?"

"You sound like a wet nurse."

"Hey, you asked. Anyway, both our lives will have to change. I've already asked for more teaching hours. And starting next year, I'll teach both semesters. The dean at Berkley has been thrilled; I'm their Indiana Jones right now. We both want a more stabilized lifestyle."

"So, no more expeditions? No more adventures?"

Logan sighs. "Finding the lost city of gold has been my life's achievement. I can be contented with that."

"And when were you planning on telling me this?"

"I'm starting a family; I thought it was obvious I won't be spending half the year traveling around the globe anymore."

Nu-uh, dude, it wasn't *obvious*, I want to scream.

"Maybe not half the year, but I thought you'd still take trips and have Winter tag along as official photographer."

"Not for the foreseeable future. Not unless something really big came along and Winter wanted to follow."

So, no more trips around the world with my best friend. My life is already changing, whether I want it to or not.

I turn to Tucker. "And what about you?"

"Yeah, a more stabilized life would be good."

"No, I was talking about the kids thing. You want them?"

Tucker shrugs. "Oh, that. Yeah, sure."

"Just like that. You don't have to think about it for even a second."

"No, I've always wanted to be a father."

At this moment I envy them their simple certainties. I wish I had some.

"Aren't you guys scared of screwing up?" I prod. "Of not being good parents? You just assume you're going to be good at it?"

"Gosh," Logan says. "You're the worst best man ever. Shouldn't you be giving calming speeches right now? Why are you trying to put doubts into my head?"

"You look calmer than a sarcophagus and clearly have no doubts."

"Because I am sure. I love Winter; I want her to be my life partner. I've longed to start a family of my own ever since—" His voice falters, and I don't need him to speak to know he's talking about losing his parents. They both died in a car accident two years after we graduated. Logan was sort of adopted by my mom ever since. He's been with us for every Christmas and Thanksgiving. And my mom is crushed they couldn't be here for the wedding, but my parents booked a cruise for this week a year in advance and would've lost all the money if they didn't go.

Adopted brother or not, I understand Logan's desire to build a home.

"I know, man," I say.

My best friend nods, shaking the sadness away. "And of course we're going to screw up, but we'll fix it, together."

I pretend to gag to lighten the mood. "You'll give me diabetes." I turn to Tucker to share a manly stare of groom-deprecating disgust, but my other friend has gone back to staring straight ahead and fidgeting.

"You, on the other hand"—I point a finger at him—"look more nervous than a bull in a china shop. What's up?"

Tucker looks at us. "Guys, I have to tell you something."

That doesn't sound promising.

"Hey, Tuck, relax," Logan says with an easy grin. "It's not like you're getting married in a few hours."

I'm less inclined to jokes, and prompt him, "Come on, man, spit it out."

"Okay." Tucker takes a deep breath. "I've made a decision... The trip to Thailand next month will be my last. Sorry, guys."

And there goes another bomb. This wedding is tearing my life apart.

Slack-jawed, I ask, "But why?"

Tucker obsessively dries his palms on his knees. "As Logan said, it's time for a more stabilized lifestyle. No more traveling around the five continents, that's all."

"What will you do? Are you going to be a Yosemite guide full time?" I ask.

"Actually..." The palm-drying pace increases. "I'm thinking of moving to LA."

And the shoe drops. "Wait, this wouldn't have anything to do with Feisty Curls, huh?"

"Who's Feisty Curls?" Logan asks.

"That actor's assistant," I explain. "Tall, curly hair, light-brown skin, green eyes." Then I point an accusing finger at Tucker. "I saw them eating each other's faces the other night."

Despite being a grown man, Tucker blushes. "I have nothing to hide," he says. "Penny and I are in love and, yes, I am going to move to LA to be closer to her."

"But what will you do for a living down there?" I ask.

Tucker takes a deep breath. "I want to open a wedding planning agency."

"You're joking," I say, just as Logan comments, "I'm so happy for you, man."

"Thanks," Tucker says to Logan, then slights me with a disdainful raise of his chin. Like a shunned milady in a regency B-movie would.

So, I backpedal a little. "What I meant is that I thought you hated planning this wedding. And you love it up here, man. You live at Yosemite when we're not somewhere on a job. And how are you going to make a wedding planning agency work in LA? The competition ought to be crushing. And all for a woman you just met?"

"Hey," Logan protests. "I hadn't known Winter much longer when I realized she was the one for me."

"Thanks." Tucker makes the hands-united-in-prayer gesture at Logan and then turns to me. "And to answer your questions. I'm in love with Penny and I want to be with her. Yes, I will miss the nature up here, but it's a sacrifice worth making. And I didn't hate planning this wedding, it was just..." He shrugs. "Different from what I'm used to. But logistics is logistics, and I think I did a pretty wonderful job." He looks at Logan for confirmation.

"Stellar, man."

"Thank you. And as for the crushing competition, Penny says a tweet from Christian praising my work will have me booked solid with brides for the next five years. And she'll help me curate my Pinterest, whatever that means, so..."

"Great to see you have it all figured out," I snap, getting up and resuming pacing around the room.

"Hey, Lover Boy," Logan calls, using my college nickname. "Why, instead of asking us a million covert questions, don't you just come out with what's really bugging you so we can discuss it openly?"

"What do you mean?"

"That all this talk of kids and commitment and whether *we*"—he points at himself and Tucker—"are ready, is more a question of you falling for a certain bridesmaid and wondering if you're ready for your first grownup relationship."

I rake a hand through my hair. "Or that."

"Sit down," Logan orders. "You're driving me nuts with all the pacing. And tell us what your dilemma is."

"It's not easy to talk to you guys, with all your certainties. You both sound so sure. Like the idea of upending your entire life for a woman isn't scary."

Logan gives me a long stare. "For the right woman, it isn't. What are you so afraid of?"

"Summer wants to get married and have kids."

Logan chuckles. "Listen, I know Winter gave you an earful yesterday. But you don't have to sound the wedding bells the moment you enter a relationship; that's not how it works."

I'm not used to *receiving* advice about women, but I need it. With a tight jaw, I say, "Enlighten me, then."

"Imagine you walked into a dating agency, or filled out a profile online. One of the first questions they'd ask is if you want to have a family, as in kids. Then they'd pair off people according to their answers. They'd never match a woman who says she wants five kids with a man who says he wants none. So, if you ticked the kids box, you'd get paired with women who'd also checked that box. But that doesn't mean you should start trying for a baby on the first night out."

"And how long do you wait?"

"There's not a fixed amount or a *right* amount of time. You date, and if you *were* to fall in love, you'd both know your relationship would *eventually* lead to getting married and starting a family. The dating world is divided into two major categories: those who want kids, and those who don't. And both categories know they should steer clear of the other, or else..."

"What if I'm not sure on which category I land?" I ask.

Logan reflects for a second and sighs. "Man, you must figure that out for yourself." He pauses. "And if I can make a suggestion? Do it before it's too late."

He means before I lose the best thing that's ever happened to me. I don't disagree.

22

SUMMER

With every passing minute, I become more nervous. The moment to move to the chapel quickly approaches, and I swear I'm more on edge than the bride. Dread at having to face Archie makes my stomach burn, and my only consolation is not being the maid of honor. A small mercy that will spare me from having to walk down the aisle arm in arm with the best man. Instead, sweet Tucker will be my escort.

I glimpse my reflection in one of the illuminated mirrors at the back of the room. At least I have my best, contoured poker face on. The makeup artist pulled off a small miracle. My cheekbones are highlighted to death, and the bluish bags under my eyes have been vanquished, while my cheeks have a healthy rose tint. And my lips shine with pink gloss. My hair is amazing, too, swept back in a romantic updo. Softly braided at the sides and collected at the nape. The style isn't too polished, with loose, curly tendrils left astray while tiny white baby's-breath flowers have been woven in strategic places. Lana's hair is the same, while Winter's is a little more elaborate, and she has ivory roses instead of baby's-breath.

The bridesmaids' gowns are out of a dream as well. Like any bridesmaid who's ever watched *27 Dresses*, I was worried my sister would pick a monstrosity. Not a period costume or a Beverly Hills fuchsia mini skirt, but she could've gone down the road of a drab olive-green color or the beaded prom dress from hell.

Instead, I'm wearing a one-shoulder illusion gown in a perfect blush shade, with soft, sweeping ruffled flanges cascading down the skirt. A smooth, shimmering sash at the waist completes the outfit.

Winter's wedding dress is next-level dreamy, though. My sister has always been the tomboy out of the two of us, but getting married has really brought out her inner Disney princess. Her gown is a caged A-line marvel covered in punched floral appliqués that start at the illusion neckline, continue to the notched bodice, and cascade down the tulle skirt. But nothing, not the hair nor the dress, can compete with the radiance of her smile.

Gosh, what it must be like to be that happy. Because no matter how perfect I look on the outside, inside, I'm slowly fading out.

A knock on the door makes me jump and causes my stomach to tie up in even more knots.

Tucker peeks his head into the room. "Ladies, are we ready to go?"

"Yes." Winter beams at him. "Where's Logan?"

"The groom is already at the altar. All the guests are seated, and Archie is waiting in the chapel's side room, from which we will make our entrance."

Even hearing his name mentioned in passing makes me want to puke.

"What about my dad?" Winter asks.

"He's with Archie. We're good to go."

Winter nods and follows Tucker out of the room.

As we're walking down a hall to reach the elevators, Lana grabs my arm, gently pulling back. "Are you okay?"

Her kind eyes are genuinely concerned, so I tell her the truth. "Right now, my biggest life's goal is not to puke on this beautiful dress."

Lana chuckles, saying, "Take this," and hands me a small wrapped candy.

"What is it?"

"Ginger. I'd gotten them in case Winter became queasy before walking down the aisle or something, but you seem to need it more than she does."

We both glance ahead of us to where Winter is bouncing down the hall in a tulle cloud. Yeah, I need the ginger more than my sister.

We take the elevator down to the lobby, reach a back exit, cross a narrow patch of garden, and stop near the side entrance to the small waiting room leading into the chapel. Everyone is supposed to go inside, but I don't want to share such a confined space with Archie, even if there'll be half a dozen other people as a buffer between us. So, I let go of Lana's arm, whispering, "You go ahead, I'll be right in."

She pulls me in for a small hug, saying, "Everything will be okay." Then she disappears inside, helping bring in Winter's train.

After a short time, the music starts. The melody streams out of the walls as if coming from the strings of a thousand violins. I count to ten. Archie and Lana must be already walking down the aisle, so I take a deep breath and walk in, taking my position at Tucker's side without meeting anyone's eyes. If my sister noticed my small cop-out, she's too busy with her own walking-down-the-aisle jitters to comment.

Tucker offers me his elbow with a warm smile. "Ready?"

I take his arm and nod.

We exit the room and reach the start of the long aisle. Before us, a white carpet runway stretches to the altar where, out of the corner of my eye, I can make out Archie's silhouette. He's tall and in a black tux, but everything else is out of focus if I don't stare at him directly, and I'd better not.

Tucker gives my arm an almost imperceptible tug, and we start our walk. I hold my head high and keep my gaze straightened ahead. I'm focusing on the forehead of the minister waiting at the center of the altar. As we pass the various rows of benches, my eyes don't stray once toward snickering ex-friends or perfect strangers, and they never drift to the right of the minister to where Archie is standing.

The best man is looking at me; I can feel his gaze burning into my skin. Archie has kept his eyes glued to me from the moment I walked into the chapel.

The closer Tucker and I get to the altar, the harder it becomes to ignore Archie's insistent stare. It's like his mere presence is exercising an irresistible pull on my soul, compelling me to look at him.

I won't look at him. I won't look at him, I chant in my head, trying to keep my resolve. But as we near the final two rows of guests, my willpower wobbles, and I give in to the inescapable tug and shift my gaze to meet his.

A mistake.

The moment our eyes lock, time ripples. It stops, while simultaneously moving faster. In the few seconds it takes me to leave Tucker's side and go take my position next to Lana, I study every detail of Archie's face. The icy-but-burning light blue of his irises. The hair, combed back in a Sunday-at-church, good-boy sweep. The soft beard that I've come to love. And the lips underneath that I yearn to kiss just one more time.

He's devastatingly handsome, and the ultimate fantasy: Archibald Hill in a black tux waiting for me at the altar. Only this is not our wedding day, and he's not here to marry me. We're just spectators to somebody else's happily ever after, while our futures head in two opposite directions.

The first notes of the wedding march fill the airy room, followed by a collective intake of breath, no doubt caused by my sister making her entrance. But I don't look away, and neither does Archie.

We're trapped in each other's stares.

23

ARCHIE

When the time finally comes to move out of the groom suite, I'm impatient. I want to see Summer, know that she's okay, and talk to her. Tucker guides us down the hall, where we make a quick stop to collect the father of the bride, and then continue outside the resort and across the garden up a small hill to the white chapel.

Tucker unlocks a door on the right-hand wall and ushers us into an even smaller, darker room than the groom suite we've been trapped in all morning. What the heck?

Logan takes a deep breath and, exchanging shoulder pats with Tucker, says, "Man, I'll see you on the other side," and moves into the church.

And now there's only Tucker, Mr. Knowles, and me left.

"Tuck," I protest. "What are we supposed to do here?"

"Wait until I go get the bridesmaids and bride," he explains, and in a petulant tone, he adds, "You'd know if you'd bothered to show for any of the meetings."

I don't reply; every word he says after "bridesmaids" washes over me like water down a waterfall. Summer will be here soon. I'll finally see her.

Tucker leaves, and the minutes tick by too slowly. To be stuck in such a tiny space with the father of the woman I'm crazy about is uncomfortable. Does he know? My guess is no. Summer's dad is too calm and contented for someone sharing the room with a man who's potentially broken his daughter's heart. If some arrogant asshole hurt my little girl, I wouldn't be so peaceful and restrained.

And just like that, I see her face. A small girl of six or seven years with a gap in her front teeth. She has Summer's long blonde hair and my mother's button nose. And I love her more than anything else in the world.

We're playing baseball in the backyard because she's a bit of a tomboy and refuses to take ballet classes like her mother would've wanted.

She laughs as she catches the ball in her leather glove and throws it back at me so quickly, I miss.

"You're too slow, Daddy," she teases and I chase her off halfway through the garden, while she squeals like a piglet, her ponytail bouncing with each step.

Then more screams break from the house because, with all our shouting, we've woken her baby brother. Summer opens the screen door and comes outside, bouncing the crying baby on her hip and scowling at us.

"Uh-oh," I say, lifting my daughter onto my shoulder and running away. "We've made Mommy angry."

With an evil smirk, Summer grabs the hose and sprinkles water down on us, making the child on her hip cackle with baby laughter.

The vision feels so real, it makes my heart beat faster, while my blood pressure drops, so much so that I have to lean against a wall for a second so I don't pass out.

"Pal, are you okay?" Mr. Knowles asks. "You look paler than the groom."

"I'm okay, Mr. Knowles, thank you," I say, hoping I have infused enough you-want-me-as-your-other-son-in-law politeness into my tone.

After what seems like an eternity, we hear female voices outside.

The door opens. Bright sunlight streams in and momentarily blinds me, before a white cloud enters the room with Winter's head sitting on top of it. The bride has to gather her skirts around her while someone helps her bring the train in from behind. Summer? I can't see.

I crane my neck, but when the figure crouching behind the bride stands up, it's Lana. No sign of Summer anywhere. Where is she?

"Archie, Lana," Tucker says. "You're up first."

No, I think, desperate. I want to see Summer before I go. But she's avoiding me. She must have waited outside. Nice try, but it won't work. I'm already trying to find a way past the bride and her skirts and out of the room when Tucker grabs my arm. "Where do you think you're going?"

"I need a minute," I say. "I'll be right back."

"No, dude." Tucker pulls me aside and lines me up next to Lana. "I've already okayed the violinists. Once the music starts, you're outta here."

As if on cue, sweet notes fill the church hall on the other side of the wall.

Lana takes my arm and looks up at me. "Ready?"

"Where's Summer?" I whisper instead of answering.

"She's right behind us," Lana whispers back. "Don't worry, you'll see her soon."

Tucker prompts us, "Okay, guys, you should go."

We exit the small chamber, take a short pause in the center of the aisle, and then make our coordinated entrance, ambling toward the altar.

Logan and the minister are already in position, waiting. I study my best friend's face. He has a rather sheepish look, that of someone who can't believe his luck. A week ago, I would've snickered at that, calling him a fool. Saying he was digging his own grave. No matter how much I liked the bride, I still thought Logan was crazy for getting married barely a year after they'd met. Well, fast forward to the present and a few *days* seems like a reasonable amount of time to decide who to spend the rest of my life with.

Lana and I reach the altar and head in opposite directions. I take my position on the right next to the groom, while she goes on the left. Logan and I clasp hands in a comradeship gesture, and then our gazes snap to the back of the church. Him, waiting for his bride; me, for my bridesmaid.

Even if I've been dying to see her all morning, when Summer makes her appearance next to Tucker I'm not prepared at all. Initially, she's hidden behind my friend and I only glimpse a flash of white-blonde hair and pink fabric. But when they reach the center of the aisle and she turns to face me... I... I fight to keep my mouth shut and not have my jaw open like the dumbstruck fool I am.

Summer is even more beautiful than usual. It must be the makeup, but her face looks like someone applied a Photoshop filter to make her skin more radiant, her lips fuller, and her eyes bigger. But to me, the most beautiful Summer will always be the one who's just woken up, hair in a tousled mess on the pillow, not an ounce of makeup on her face, and a little secret smile on her lips that I put there the night before.

Now, she isn't smiling. And it's my fault.

To a casual observer, she'd appear fine, but I know better and can read the minor details. Like the tautness of her jaw. The slight downward curve of her mouth. And her eyes, which would usually fight to find me in a room, turned away.

Her stare is pointed straight ahead, and so lifeless it might as well belong to a robot.

Please look at me, I chant in my head as she walks toward me. Come on, look up. Look at me.

When I'm about to lose hope she'll meet my gaze, her eyes lock on mine and it's the most powerful sensation I've ever experienced. My stomach drops as if I were free-falling, my head spins, and my heart beats so fast it might jump out of my rib cage and go prostrate itself at her feet. Is this what being in love feels like?

No, I prefer thinking that to be in love is to lie in bed next to the other person without a care in the world and wishing you were nowhere else. It's having my heart jump in my throat because a message from her has arrived when I wasn't expecting it. Or counting the minutes until a stupid bachelor party will be over so I can run back to her. Or feeling like the luckiest man on Earth whenever she kisses me.

What I'm experiencing right now isn't love; it's fear, pure and primal. A cold dread that I've ruined everything with my indecision.

Winter reaches the altar. I didn't even notice the bride make her entrance, and I spot her now only because she cuts into my view of her sister. Logan hurries to take Winter's hand. A goofy, what-did-I-do-to-deserve-you smile stamped on his lips. And for the second time in a few minutes, I can't help but think, *You lucky bastard.*

The bride and groom reach their positions at the altar and free my vision field again. I'm worried Summer might have dropped her gaze, but her eyes are there, waiting for me, giving me hope.

All I need is a second chance, and I won't screw up this time.

24

SUMMER

The ceremony is romantic and sweet.

The groom is dashing in his tux, and sure and calm as he professes his undying love for the woman standing by his side. Only a trace of happy tears glistens in his eyes, giving away the depth of his emotions.

The bride's voice trembles the slightest bit while she's in the middle of her vows, but she recovers quickly and, with a resplendent smile, is able to finish without crying.

The guests follow the celebration of love in moved silence while the mother of the bride's sobs can be heard in the background.

The only hiccup comes when the best man has to be nudged by his fellow groomsman to bring the rings forward. Apparently, he was too busy staring at one of the bridesmaids—*me*—to realize his big moment had come.

How do I feel about it all?

So confused.

Weddings are too emotional. I shouldn't be forced to reflect on my love life while attending one.

The way Archie is staring at me, he could ask me to be his casual fling for the rest of our lives and I'd gladly say yes. That's why I have to avoid him at all costs. Tomorrow morning the party will be over. Winter and

Logan will go on their honeymoon. My parents will head back to Pasadena. And Archie will be off to Berkley, out of my life for good. I have to resist for twenty-four hours, tops. I can do it.

It's easy to avoid him in the melee that follows the happy couple out of the chapel. Two groups form outside, ready to throw rice at the bride and groom as they exit the church. I make sure Archie and I are on opposite sides.

Before moving to the reception, we have to pose for a few pictures. But it's all very orchestrated: bridesmaids on one side, groomsmen on the other, now only the bride and bridesmaids, groom and groomsmen, let's switch it up, bring the parents in, and we're done. No occasion to talk.

Next, the reception. The weather has been nice, allowing for lunch to be served outside.

The party will take place on a portion of the estate opposite the vineyard. This patch of green, short-cut lawn is enclosed by tall, majestic trees —a clearing in a magical forest straight out of a storybook. The seating area has been staged to perfection: a rectangular raised stage under a white pole structure resembling a house with no walls. Crystal chandeliers dangle from the high middle pole, and white canvas with wide gaps between them serve as a roof. Long, rectangular tables fill the entire space, each decorated with green and white flower centerpieces and lined by King Louis XVI chairs with an oval back, white upholstery, and a natural wooden structure.

It's what I imagine happily ever after looks like, which only serves to remind me why Archie and I can't be together. Because I want this for myself one day. Not the fabled wedding, or to be the princess at the ball. But what comes next. The feet rubs at the end of a long day, the movie nights with takeout, lazy Sunday mornings spent in bed making love, the spontaneous weekend trips, the dinners cooked side by side, and all the sweet nothings exchanged in between. I want to share all my sunrises and sunsets with that special person who knows every ugly detail of me and still loves me unconditionally. I want a man who loves me so completely he wants to spend the rest of his life with me, and not be afraid to pledge that love in front of all our friends and family.

Family. That's the other, more important reason. I want one of my own. A husband. Kids. The white fence. And the cat—no offense to dog lovers.

And Archie can give me none of those things. We're Monica and Richard from *Friends;* I want kids, he doesn't. I just have to be strong and stay away from him and hope one day my Chandler will come along.

Just another few hours. I can be strong.

The seating arrangements are on my side. Inside the wall-less house, the wedding party table is laid parallel to the short side of the rectangular dais while the other tables are perpendicular to it. The bride and groom are seated in the middle. Archie is on Logan's right, and I'm on my sister's side two spots down. Unless I lean forward, I can't even see the best man, which is great.

I've been so lost inside my head that it isn't until the second starter that I notice the person sitting next to me. And I notice him only because he asks me if I could pass him the breadbasket.

I mean, I knew Lana had a plus one, and who the plus one was. But how the hell did I not notice I've been sitting next to Christian Slade for the past half hour? I swear he wasn't here when I sat down and, okay, I've been doing my best to stare the other way, but Penelope, his assistant, must've conjured him out of thin air.

I hand him the breadbasket, trying not to blush. And not because he's the celebrity actor who I've had a crush on since his first movie came out. But because this is the man who found Lana crying in a hotel closet after she'd discovered the affair I was having with her boyfriend.

With every new person I meet that knows about The Mistake, fresh shame engulfs me, and I'm brought back to that dark spot in my past filled only with self-loathing.

He takes the breadbasket from me and nods a thanks. "Summer, right?" he says.

I nod.

"I'm Christian," he says, needlessly.

"Er... nice to meet you?" It comes out as a question because I'm not clear where this man's opinion of me lands. Also, we both have our hands full—his with a bread bun, and mine with the knife and fork I've just picked up—so we don't have to shake.

Christian breaks off a piece of bread without bringing it to his mouth. "I always wondered how I'd feel about meeting you."

He has been wondering about me? I'm too stunned to reply, so he continues. "On one hand, you hurt Lana in a way no one deserves to be hurt." A wave of humiliation hits me as Christian speaks, and I lower my gaze in response. "On the other, if it weren't for you, I would've never met her..."

As per my new policy of not shying away from my mistakes, I own up to them. "What I did to her was inexcusable. And I don't know where she found the strength to forgive me. I'm only glad something good came out of the mess I made. She's really happy with you, and all I ask is that you give me the benefit of the doubt."

Before he can reply, Lana pops her head forward.

"Hey, what are you two whispering about?"

Christian lowers his tone even further. "I was asking Summer for skin-care advice." Now I'm even more stunned that Christian Slade, *People's* Magazine Sexiest Man Alive six times in a row, knows what I do for a living. "I have to beat Hollywood's ageism, ya know?"

Lana rolls her eyes. "Don't worry, your skin is more glowing than mine." She wrinkles her nose and, looking at me, she adds, "So annoying."

When Lana turns away again, Christian gives me a small, imperceptible nod that I receive as, "You get the benefit of the doubt once, but hurt my girl again and you'll end up on my shit list forever."

I nod back, projecting, "Thank you, and I won't screw up again, I've learned my lesson."

* * *

The second course is cleared out and, before the wedding cake is presented, it's time for the speeches. Logan makes an impossibly romantic one that has half the audience crying. My sister takes the mic next. She spends the first half of her speech gushing over her new hubby, making everyone aww—more tears are shed. Then she turns to Mom and Dad and thanks them. And then she turns to me.

"And, Summer, thank you for being here by my side this week. I know

I'm not always the easiest sister to have, that sometimes"—she raises her eyes to the sky as if the next phrase is costing her a lot—"I butt my nose into stuff that is really none of my business. And sometimes I have too strong opinions..."

Logan coughs loudly, and the crowd laughs.

"My husband seems to agree," she says, and then looks back at me. "But please know that when I'm at my most insufferable self, it is only because I love you and I want the best for you. You're an amazing human being, inside and out, and I hope you know that."

I feel a lump form in my throat as I nod at her. But she's not finished. "You've always been there for me, through thick and thin, when the opposite hasn't always been true, and there's nothing I regret more. But we're both just humans and we make mistakes, and if people can't move past that"—she pointedly stares at Daria and Susan— "that's their loss. You deserve love and you deserve happiness, and I hope that one day you'll be as lucky as I feel today to have found a man who loves you as thoroughly and completely as you deserve." She makes to sit down but then stands up again and adds, "And that he won't be too much of a chicken to fight for you when the time comes."

The crowd laughs and claps as my sister pointedly passes the microphone to Archie.

And then it's the best man's turn to speak. I'm still so emotional from my sister's speech I'm not sure I'm prepared to hear his sexy voice magnified by a thousand speakers.

Archie stands up, giving me an excuse to watch him while he can't stare back for longer than a few moments, not unless he wants to make his speech very awkward.

Still, our eyes lock before he begins his address to the crowd. "Logan and I have known each other since we were eighteen and by some lucky twist of fate ended up sharing a freshman dorm room. I have to say, when I first stepped inside and saw this prepped-up kid in his ironed shirt, he was so prim I wondered if he pressed his pajamas, too, and if we could ever become friends."

Archie pauses and frowns theatrically, allowing the audience to chuckle at his engaging anecdote. "Luckily, as the days passed, his stock of home-ironed clothes ran out and his gear became as crumpled and wrinkled as that of any other respectable college kid." Another short pause to collect laughs. "But what sealed the deal was when I came home the week after orientation and found him sleeping on his bed with his mouth open and drooling on the pillow, a bag of Doritos at his side, crumbs all around him, and his white T-shirt stained by the orange imprint of many fingertips. That's when I knew we could be friends for life."

More laughs. Gosh, I hate that he's such a showman and that everyone in the room is eating out of his hand. Especially the ladies, I can't help but notice, with a bitter aftertaste in my mouth. If he wants to substitute me for someone else, he'll have his pick tonight. A snap of the fingers and they'll all fall at his feet, just like I did. But it's not his fault for being who he is. I'd been warned and chose to ignore the alarm bells. If I have to deal with a broken heart right now, I've no one to blame but myself.

"I guess for Winter and Logan it's been the same," Archie carries on. "Not a case of love at first sight here, folks." The people in the audience who know about Winter and Logan's insta-hate past laugh, including me. The first time my sister described the groom to me, she called him Satan.

"But it didn't take them much to discover they shared more than they initially thought," Archie continues. "Only the archeological discovery of the century, being trapped in an ancient tomb together, escaping a bunch of trigger-happy lunatics through the jungle, and having to save my life along with that of everybody else on that expedition. Easy, right? Well, not exactly, because my boneheaded friend almost blew it at this point"—Archie stares at me, making a breath catch in my throat—"by not saying how he really felt."

His gaze lingers on me for another second before moving away, and I can breathe again. "He could've lost her, but, thankfully, only two international flights later, he managed to right his mistake and profess his undying love. I wasn't there to witness the event, but I was told begging was involved." Again, everyone laughs. "And now here we are. Logan, my friend, today you're the luckiest man on Earth to have convinced this amazing woman to be with you for the rest of your lives. I wish you joy and happiness, and that your love will go on as strong as today until the end of time." He stares at me again. "I would consider myself ever so lucky to convince a woman to love me for all eternity, just like you have Winter."

The crowd awws, and a few hopeless romantic tears are shed around the room. While I'm positive I'm about to die. What did he mean by that? Has he changed his mind? No, I can't tell myself stories; people don't simply change overnight.

"And before I begin to sound too much like a movie soundtrack, I'd better wrap this up." Archie raises his champagne flute. "To the bride and groom."

The audience explodes with booming applause.

25

SUMMER

I cruise through the cutting of the cake unscathed. The traditional moment takes place in a spot further down the lawn where the cake is awaiting Winter and Logan under a gazebo—a wrought-iron structure covered in green leaves and white flowers, following the same theme as the other flower arrangements. Again, there are enough people around to ensure a big buffer between Archie and me. With the guests forming a large semicircle around the gazebo, I can hide in the crowd and follow the event from the sidelines.

Distances, however, thin considerably as we head to the dance floor—back in the wall-less house where tables have been removed to clear a space in its center—for the first dance.

But being demoted to simple bridesmaid has the added benefit of me being paired with Tucker for the last of the wedding party's duties. And if I sneak off stage the second the song is over, I can disappear into the crowd again and not have to face Archie.

With this determination in mind, I find Tucker, steer him to the opposite side of the dance floor to where Lana and Archie are standing, and wait for the first song to start. The notes of Ed Sheeran's "Perfect" soon fill the air, and I have to work hard at keeping the waterworks in check as my sister and Logan walk onstage hand in hand and begin to waltz. The bride and groom can't take their eyes off each other, and they look so unabashedly happy my chest tightens.

And then I make my first mistake; I look up and find Archie's eyes, and my heart squeezes even harder.

The first chorus ends, our cue to enter the dance floor. Tucker and I join hands and I let him lead. As my dancing partner twirls me around, my eyes search for those of the man who has stolen my soul. We meet and lose each other's gazes again at each turn in a vortex of emotions until the song ends.

My plan to flee forgotten, I remain on the dance floor, breathless, staring at him. Tucker leaves me to go grab Penny from the crowd and lead her on for the second dance. Similarly, all other couples break apart and reshuffle. Winter is to dance with our father, Logan with Mom. And when Christian claims Lana for himself, the best man is free to close the distance between us, imprison my body in his arms, and spin me to the center of the stage.

"All of Me" from John Legend begins to play next.

Why did my sister have to pick the most romantic songs on the planet?

My heart can't take any more strong emotions; it's already been battered and crushed too many times. I'm so ruinously in love with this man holding me, it's ridiculous. I can't bear the thought of having to say goodbye to him tomorrow. Of never seeing him again. I search Archie's eyes for a clue he feels the same, and his gaze seems to promise everything his mouth still hasn't said.

A small flame of hope lurks in my chest, but I squash it down. I can't get carried away again. For all I know, this could be just a beautiful goodbye for him.

The song ends and, before I can do or say anything, Archie scoops me up into his arms and carries me off the dance floor and over to a wooden bench hidden in the trees surrounding the lawn.

I'm holding on to him, my fingers laced behind his neck. And as we sit down, I don't let go. Archie sits and scoots me closer to him with one arm, while his other hand moves up to cup my cheek.

Eyes as intense as ever, he whispers, "I love you, Summer, and I'm not ready to let you go. Whatever it takes."

For a moment, the words catch in my throat and I can't speak. I gulp down a sob, and, in a trembling voice, I say, "I love you, too. But—"

Archie presses a finger to my mouth. "No buts."

I free one of my hands from behind his neck and put it over the hand covering my mouth. I kiss his fingertips and push the hand down, saying, "But because I love you, I can't force you into something you don't want. Even if we could make it work at first, one of us would have to go against our wishes in the end. And I would never do that to someone I love."

"Summer, I've been stupid. I had no idea what I wanted before I met you. I've never been in love before. I've never felt like I'd die if I had to be apart from someone, away from you." He taps my nose. "I always thought marriage wasn't for me, that I would never find a woman I needed by my side every day, but you are that woman, Summer Knowles."

"How can you be sure? How can you change your mind so radically in just a week?"

Archie bows his head for a second as if to collect his thoughts, then raises his gaze again. "In the past, I've never felt anything more than a fleeting attraction for the women I've been with. And even in the strongest cases, it burned away quickly, a few weeks at most—"

"We haven't known each other for more than a week." I'm being pushy, but if I'm going to open my heart again, I need to be positive he means what he's saying. Because he's the one man who could crush my soul so thoroughly there would be no coming back. "How can you be sure this will be any different? That your infatuation won't just disappear?"

"Because yesterday"—he puts a hand over his chest—"when you left me at the restaurant, I was in physical pain. I couldn't breathe, Summer, not being able to hold you, to kiss you." He emphasizes the need with a brief touch of his lips on mine. "It drove me crazy. I've never felt that way about anyone or anything. I can't lose you."

"But last night—"

Archie scoffs, interrupting me. "Last night we had exactly two conversations. You were unreasonable for the first one, and a randy drunk for the second."

I gasp in mock offense. "Who are you calling a randy drunk?"

The best man grins. "Hey, I'll take randy over sad or angry any day."

I hide my face in the nook of his shoulder. "How can you still want to be with me after the way I behaved?"

"Because I love you, all of you. I love unreasonable you. I love randy drunk you. And I love regular you most of all. Listen, I know it won't be super easy right off the bat. I will have to find a job in LA—"

This time it's me silencing him with a hand over his mouth. I search his eyes again for any sign this is a trick, but only find sincerity in them. "You've really thought about this. You'd give up your job for me?"

I lower my hand so he can speak.

Archie scratches the back of his head. "To be honest, the way things are going I'll need to find a new job soon, anyway. Tucker is quitting next month. And Logan will cut back on his travels as soon as his work in Thailand is complete. And if he's not with me, I'm done, too. Wouldn't be the same."

Doubts assail me again. "Is that what this is? Your life is falling apart, and you're getting attached to me as an anchor?"

"No, no, no, and no. I'm in love with you, and even if everything stayed the same, I'd move to LA in a heartbeat."

"That's a pity," I say, and his face falls. So I smirk, and add, "Because I don't want to stay in LA. There's nothing left for me there." Archie's eyes shine with hope again. "I started looking for jobs in San Francisco the moment Winter told me she was moving up here."

"Really?"

"Yeah, I have a couple of interviews scheduled for next week."

He pulls me closer and kisses me again. "So, it's settled; you can move in with me. I rent a studio apartment, but we can search for something bigger or closer to your office once you find a new job. We can find a yoga studio and keep doing Acro together. And I can't wait to show you all my favorite places in Berkley and San Francisco. It's perfect."

Almost, I think. Because so far we've talked about everything except the most important question.

I brace myself, and ask, "What about kids?"

Archie goes a little rigid underneath me; I'm still sitting on his lap, and my body stiffens in response.

With the hand that's not wrapped around my waist, he pushes away a loose strand of hair from my forehead. "For the first time in my life, I can see myself as a father. I don't know, all this time I thought I was incapable of love. And if I couldn't fall in love with a woman how could I ever start a family? But with you, I even imagined what she'd look like."

"Who?"

"Our daughter." My heart starts a raging pounding in my chest. "She'd have your hair and my mother's nose. She'd be as smart as her mother and as much of a troublemaker as her father. And if we had a boy instead, he'd still be brilliant. And we would love both of them with all our hearts." He pauses, a slight frown on his face. "Can I make a request though?"

I nod.

"I've researched the whole IVF thing, and I'm not a fan. Can we make the babies the old-fashioned way?"

"You've researched IVF?" A single tear rolls down my cheek. "Is this for real?"

"What do I have to do to convince you, you stubborn woman?" He groans in frustration and settles me on the bench next to him. "Drop to one knee?" Archie bends to the ground and takes hold of both my hands. "Summer Knowles, will you—"

Before he can finish, I use our joined hands to pull him back onto the bench. "You don't have to propose right away!"

"Hey, I was grand-gesturing you. Are you sure you don't want all this?" He waves at the wedding set-up in the distance. "The fairy-tale wedding, the happily ever after?"

"Of course I do, but today, *happy for now* is more than enough. All I needed was to be sure that if we started dating, you'd be open to marriage and a family... one day."

He frowns at me. "*Happy for now*? Is that a new thing?"

I smile. "Not a fan of romance novels, huh?"

He makes a *duh* face.

"Happy for now is where happily ever afters are born. When todays turn into tomorrows and all days afterward."

Archie stands up and pulls me along, pressing my body against his. "I'll take the now thing, Summer Knowles, but be ready because I plan on getting all those tomorrows."

"Good," I say, and close my eyes as my Prince Charming kisses me.

EPILOGUE
SUMMER

Some forty years later – Christmas Day

"What time are the little goblins arriving?" my husband asks, dropping the potato peels into the trash.

I look up from the stove where I'm stirring the cranberry sauce. "Should be here soon."

Archie straightens up and kisses me on the side of the neck. "And how many of the little monsters are we having over this year?"

"Nine," I say. "And don't pretend you can't remember how many grand-kids you have; I know you love each of them to pieces."

Archie chuckles. "Of course I do. They're the best parts of us."

I turn off the stove and wrap my arms behind his neck. I smile, feeling a warmth spread through my chest. It's hard to believe that we've been married for over thirty years now and that the love and happiness we share has only grown stronger.

I kiss my husband, and he returns the kiss with the same passion that never faded over the years.

"If my back was still what it used to be," he whispers in my ear. "I'd lift that pretty behind of yours onto the kitchen island and—"

The doorbell rings, interrupting whatever scandalous thing he was about to say.

"Easy tiger." I playfully swat him with a wooden spoon. "You don't want to traumatize the kids."

He smirks. "They're grown adults and at the rate they're reproducing, I doubt I have anything left to teach them."

I chuckle. "You might have a point."

We both make our way down the hall to greet our children and grand-children with open arms. As the house fills with laughter, love, and the smell of Christmas dinner, I can't help but think back to that day at the edge of the vineyards when Archie and I talked about our future. We had no idea what was in store for us, but we knew that we had each other, that we wanted to make the journey together, and that was enough.

Looking at our family now, the love that radiates off of us is palpable, a blanket of warmth that wraps around me and cocoons me in pure content-ment. The joy that we have shared and continue to share together is like a fire, engulfing us with its blazing light and heat, seeping into every crevice of our hearts. Archie was right, we've had our fair share of tomorrows, and with each passing day, our love only grows stronger. It has never wavered, even when life got tough. And for that, I'll be forever grateful.

I sneak a glance at my husband, who's playing with our youngest grandchild. He catches my eye and winks at me, and my stomach flips— no matter that I'm old and a grandma, that man still makes me feel like a blushing bridesmaid. Same as that first week when he stole my heart and soul.

Over the racket, I call out for everyone to get ready to eat. As we sit down to dinner, I look around the table at the faces of the people I love most in the world laughing and talking animatedly. My heart fills with joy and gratitude once again, knowing that no matter what happens in the years to come, we'll always have these moments to carry us through.

The meal is a whirlwind of happy chaos. Followed by even more pande-monium as we gather around the tree to open the presents. As the kids play with their new, shiny toys, the adults watch a family movie together as is tradition, gathered around the fireplace. And when the little ones begin to fall asleep in their parents' arms, our children—we ended up having four, two boys and two girls—one by one get up and return to their own happy homes.

Once everyone is gone, the house is a mess. Archie grabs a gigantic trash bag and starts collecting all the wayward wrapping paper. I grab his hand and make him stop. "Leave it," I say. "We'll take care of it tomorrow."

"Are you sure?"

I wrap my arms around his neck and sink my fingers into his silky white hair. "Yes. Let's go to bed."

He drops his forehead to mine. "Yes, my love."

I move up the stairs first, and he gives me a playful spank on the behind like I knew he would.

I laugh and turn around to face him, my heart full of love as always. "You're incorrigible."

He grins, his eyes twinkling mischievously. "You love it."

"I do," I say, leaning in to kiss him. "I love everything about you."

We make our way into our bedroom, still chuckling at each other's jokes and teasing. As we slip into bed and snuggle close, I can't help but think about how lucky I am to have found my soulmate all those years ago. Even after all this time, he still makes me feel like the most beautiful, cherished woman in the world.

Archie grabs my hand over the covers and kisses my knuckles. "You think we've earned that happily ever after yet?"

I raise an eyebrow. "Why? You plan on dying on me soon?"

"Hell, no, I plan on annoying you until you get old and crusty."

"I already am old and crusty."

"Oh, please, you still look like a springy sixty-year-old."

I laugh at his compliment. "And you still act like a teenage boy."

Archie grins, his eyes glinting with mischief. "Well, that's because you always keep me young and agile."

I shake my head but can't help the smile that spreads across my face. "To answer your question, no, I think we're still in a happy-for-now phase. You still have a few decades of happiness to give me, mister."

"Good," he murmurs, his hand stroking my hair. "Because I plan on giving you a lifetime of happiness, missus."

Archie yawns and drops his head on the pillow, reaching under the covers to pull me closer. My head rests on his chest. I close my eyes and listen to the sound of his heartbeat. As we drift off to sleep, arms wrapped tightly around each other, I know that whatever the future may bring our way, we'll face it together with unwavering love and devotion. For Archie and me, there will always be another tomorrow.

AUTHOR'S NOTE

Dear Reader,

I hope you enjoyed reading *The Love Proposal*. I had so much fun writing this book and expanding it to make the story even more swoon-worthy with the help of the amazing team at my publisher, Boldwood Books.

This book is very special to me, not only because of the gorgeous Viking who stole my writer's heart in the previous story and earned a HEA (or HFN?!) of his own, but also because I poured a little of myself into this story.

The opening scene might've felt weird for a rom-com. I debated for a long time the choice to make the book start in a sterile and cold hospital room. But, if you've been following me for a while, you might already know that my son was born through IVF. Before starting that long process with my husband, I had no idea how it worked, and halfway through, I'm not going to lie, the harvesting needle sounded scary as hell.

In the end, for me, it was a very positive, non-painful experience that I wanted to share in a fun way in my writing. If you're struggling with infertility or just want to give yourself more time to make a decision about motherhood like Summer, feel free to write to me if you have any questions. I can't give any medical advice, but I can share my personal experience of IVF with you.

Now, to move on to more bookish topics. The next book in the series, *Love to Hate You*, will feature Samantha Baker as our lead lady. You might remember her as Christian's favorite movie producer from *The Love Theorem*. She's a posh city girl and hates being away from New York. So, of course, evil little me, I'm going to send her to the country to supervise the off-track production of Christian's latest small-town rom-com. Emerald Creek doesn't have a Starbucks, and no one knows how to make a decent cocktail. But the town does have a frustratingly gorgeous cowboy Travis, the source of all of Samantha's problems, who she can't get out of her head no matter how hard she tries.

Now, I have to ask you a big favor. If you loved my story, please consider leaving a review on your favorite retailer's website, on Goodreads, or wherever you like to post reviews (your blog, BookTok, in a text to your best friend...). Reviews are the best gift you can give to an author, and word of mouth is the most powerful means of book discovery.

Thank you for your constant support!

Camilla, x

MORE FROM CAMILLA ISLEY

We hope you enjoyed reading *The Love Proposal*. If you did, please leave a review.

If you'd like to gift a copy, this book is also available as an ebook, paperback, large print, digital audio download and audiobook CD.

Sign up to Camilla Isley's mailing list for news, competitions and updates on future books.

https://bit.ly/CamillaIsleyNews

Discover fun-filled romantic comedies from Camilla Isley...

ABOUT THE AUTHOR

Camilla Isley is an engineer who left science behind to write bestselling contemporary rom-coms set all around the world. She lives in Italy.

Visit Camilla's website: https://camillaisley.com

Follow Camilla Isley on social media:

instagram.com/camillaisley

tiktok.com/@camilla.isley

facebook.com/camillaisley

twitter.com/camillaisley

bookbub.com/authors/camilla-isley

youtube.com/RomanceAudiobooks

Boldwood

Boldwood Books is an award-winning fiction publishing company seeking out the best stories from around the world.

Find out more at www.boldwoodbooks.com

Join our reader community for brilliant books, competitions and offers!

Follow us
@BoldwoodBooks
@BookandTonic

Sign up to our weekly
deals newsletter

https://bit.ly/BoldwoodBNewsletter

Ingram Content Group UK Ltd.
Milton Keynes UK
UKHW041832240723
425716UK00002B/10